Who is She?

A Viv Fraser Mystery

V. Clifford

Inverardoch Press

Published by Inverardoch Press

Also by V.Clifford

The Viv Fraser Mysteries:

Beyond Cutting

Finding Tess

Digging up the Dead

Deception is the Old Black

Non Fiction

Freud's Converts

Chapter One

Wednesday

The flat was hot and stuffy. Her mum belonged to that post-war generation who really did believe that cleanliness was next to godliness and that fresh air was the cure for everything, but today the cocktail of chemicals in the guise of violets and spring flowers had nowhere to escape to. Viv glanced around at the windows, all secured. Very unlike her mum. Fair enough. Edinburgh was known for its formidable east wind and today it was on the wrong side of biting, but still, the flat could do with a serious airing.

'Mum. Did you hear me? I think he's probably the same guy and you've just forgotten.'

Her mum sat in her usual chair picking at the edges of her nails. 'No. I have not forgotten. The man that usually cleans the windows is bald and this one had a full head of hair. So unless I'm losing my marbles it was a different man.'

Viv, who uncharitably thought the latter was entirely possible, said, 'Okay. What do you want me to do?'

Her mum paused and screwed up her eyes as if dredging her memory. She shook her head and blew out a breath. 'No. It won't come. But just you watch your back.'

Viv's eyebrows reached for her hairline. 'Right. I'll get away now. I'm sure Mand will be here later with James.'

Her mum's face transformed from exasperation to adoration in a single motion. Viv marvelled at how many muscles it took to do that and how lovely her mum looked when she was happy. She rubbed her mum's arm and went to the door, stopped and glanced back. 'D'you want me to put the TV on or open a window?' As if the two were connected.

Her mum shook her head, and said, 'I'm perfectly capable . . . You just mind your back.'

'Sure mum, see you later.'

'Sure. How much later?'

Ah, not so out of sorts as to forget the customary dig. Amanda, Viv's sister, was the golden girl, the regular visitor. And now with James she was more popular than ever. Viv buttoned up her jacket and wrapped her scarf round her neck as she approached her car. She stopped abruptly and hissed through gritted teeth at the sight of a white illegal-to-park-here sticker plastered over the driver's section of the windscreen. 'Shit! Shit! Shit!' It wasn't the first time the warden of her mum's sheltered accommodation had been overzealous. She knew Viv's car, but when she was idle, which she seemed to be too often, she took pleasure in making life difficult for others. Not an ideal trait for a carer. Viv started scraping it off but the adhesive was solid and it took a few swipes with the screen wash before she'd cleared enough of the windscreen to see to drive.

'Bitch!' she mouthed at the warden, who was standing with arms crossed glaring out of the window of her own flat. Viv wondered about this vindictive streak and how it translated into the lives of the residents. One of these days she'd report her.

It took fifteen minutes to drive home to the West Bow. What did her mum mean with all that 'mind your back' stuff? She was many things, but a conspiracy theorist wasn't one of them. And why no TV today? Viv couldn't remember the last time she'd been in her mum's flat when the TV was off. Also she never had the windows closed. The merits of fresh air had been drummed into them as kids although the cleaning smells that Viv remembered from childhood were Lysol and polish, almond polish. She made a mental note to have a conversation with Mand about it, but it would have to wait until she was in the right mood. Tricky to gauge.

She checked her mailbox in the front passage of the stair. Nothing but junk. Viv bolted upstairs two at a time, arriving at her door slightly out of breath. Her doormat was pitched up against the wall and the landing was damp. She remembered it was Wednesday, the day that the stair cleaners came, when it suited them. What was going on today? Even her stairwell smelled of disinfectant. If only she'd remembered she'd have stayed away. Her key was poised over the lock when Ronnie from next door poked his head out, as usual avoiding eye contact with her.

He said, 'Eh Viv, you've had a visitor.'

'Really?' She wasn't expecting anyone and few people knew her home address.

'Yes, a man. Tall, handsome stranger, I suppose you'd say.' He bit the inside of his cheek.

She was intrigued. 'Did he say who he was or what he wanted?'

'No. I was just getting my coat on when I heard your letter box . . . snap shut, and I wondered who would walk all the way up those stairs when there's a place for post in the entrance hall . . . I was on my way out, not being nosy.'

Viv shook her head. Ronnie was the perfect neighbour. She hardly knew he was there, but at times like this he was a valuable ally. 'What did he look like?'

Ronnie glanced over his shoulder as if to check that no one could hear him and lowered his voice. 'I probably shouldn't say this but he looked Germanic, Teutonic. He made me think of Wagner.' This was as fluent as she'd heard him in a long while. Conversations were not his thing. His speech impediment held him back with strangers, but perhaps he was becoming more at ease with her.

The description wasn't of anyone familiar to her but she smiled at the idea of Ronnie being a fan of Wagner. She'd never heard music from his flat that indicated a passion for anything other than modern jazz. She unlocked her door and glanced behind it. Nothing there. 'How odd. I don't know anyone particularly tall. Was he blonde?'

Ronnie nodded, 'But not flaxen.'

This also made Viv smile, 'And handsome? Nope, definitely not anyone that would come to my flat. Thanks for letting me know.'

They both stepped over their own thresholds. Viv's interest piqued by the idea of a stranger, as Ronnie said, coming all the way up to her door when he'd have found out that she wasn't at home by buzzing from down at street level. Did he want to leave something but was interrupted by Ronnie? Maybe he was at the wrong door, or just wanted to see exactly where she lived. Well, if he wanted to speak to her badly he'd turn up again.

The light on Viv's answering machine flashed. She hit the play button and sat down at her desk waiting for the message. The sound of Jinty's husky voice immediately improved her mood.

'Hi, Viv. I know you don't really do this kind of thing but I wondered as a complete one off, I mean complete one off, you might squeeze in an extra trim? We have a composer staying and he hasn't had time to have his hair cut before his performance tomorrow night, and I thought since you were coming here anyway you might blah blah. You know the form. Ring me.' Her voice lowered to just above a whisper as if she was worried about being heard, 'Wouldn't matter two hoots if you can't do it. I mean really, who goes on tour and forgets to have their hair cut?' Her voice returned to its original formality. 'Completely understand. Looking forward.'

Viv nibbled her lip. She knew Jinty well and there was more to this message than the words suggested. What was she trying to tell her? Also it was a long message for Jinty, who hated speaking to machines almost as much as Viv did. Equally unusual for her to ask a favour, so there must be something going on. Viv rubbed her hands together then checked her diary. She couldn't refuse Jinty anything unless it was impossible. She glanced at her laptop then quickly tapped out an email replying to Jinty.

She had a pile of things to do but couldn't concentrate to do anything that mattered. Sal's flight wasn't until 6pm but she had to be at the airport by 4.30 at the latest, which meant leaving the West Bow at 3.30. She put a washing in the machine, went to the loo, stacked the crockery from the draining board away in cupboards. She flinched when the phone rang, and gave herself a telling-off. By the time she reached the sitting-room the light on the answering machine was already blinking. She pressed the play button. The sound of a telephone handset hitting against its cradle and her mum cursing to herself at the other end before hanging up was all she heard. What could she want? Viv had only just seen her. She called her back. No answer. She tried Amanda's number but it went straight to voicemail. Her mum was no idle chatterer so only used the telephone if she had something important to say. She was about to pick up her bag and head back to her mum's flat when her mobile vibrated. Her sister.

'Mand, how is mum? She just tried to ring here but obviously got bored untangling the cord of her phone. I'm going online right now to buy her a cordless phone.'

'That's a waste of money. You know she hates the telephone. Nothing will make her leave a message unless it's an absolute emergency. But never mind that. How was she when you were here earlier? I've come down to the lobby to ring you.'

Viv didn't want to say exactly how she'd been, since Mand loved a drama and would blow the slightest thing out of proportion. 'She was fine. Why?'

'She keeps telling me to mind my back.'

The sound of heavy traffic, then a siren at Mand's end, made it impossible for their conversation to continue. Viv shuffled papers on her desk until it passed.

'I can't think what's riled her. She said the same to me. But, Mand, you know she's getting a bit forgetful.'

Mand sighed. 'Oh you always say that. She's fine. Did she tell you about the window cleaner?'

Viv raised her eyebrows. 'Yes she did mention that.'

'She's right, Viv. I've just checked with the warden and the window cleaner isn't due for another month. Whoever it was, was casing the joint.'

This had already crossed Viv's mind but she still didn't want Mand to go off on one. 'There must be . . . actually let's leave it. If they were after something in mum's flat they'll return. Now that we know we can make sure the warden keeps a closer eye.'

'Well that's just it, the warden did see him and has CCTV of the car he came in. You'll have to go and see her. She'll show you what she's got. She just brushed me off with 'too busy.'.'

The idea of having to speak to the woman, who'd already cost her an extra fifteen minutes scraping white gloopy paper off her windscreen this morning, wasn't on the cards anytime soon, but she said, 'Sure I can do that.'

As if Mand had caught something in Viv's tone she said, 'You won't do it, will you. This is another thing that I'll have to take on. James . . .'

Viv interrupted her, 'I said I'd do it.'

Mand, a mistress of emotional blackmail, had had such a different relationship with their mother that Viv sometimes wondered if they were sisters at all. Family photograph albums contained impressive evidence that they were, but they even looked so different it seemed impossible.

'In fact I'm on my way. I'll keep you posted.'

'You always say that and never do.'

This wasn't true but the usual chain of events when it was to do with their mum went something like, Mand asked Viv to do something, Viv thought Mand was overreacting but got worn down enough to take action anyway, Mand would keep phoning and leaving messages to see if Viv had followed through, and on one of those calls Viv would fill her in, so the need to ring her back to fill her in didn't occur, because Mand always interrupted the sequence and got her information before Viv had had time to think it through. This often meant that Viv either withheld a load of info, or just spilled whatever she had and let Mand do what she did best, go off on one.

Viv decided to jog back to her mum's to fill in some of the anxious time before picking up Sal. That way she'd avoid being wound up by the overzealous warden sticking another of those notices on her windscreen again. She trotted down through the Grassmarket, along King's Stables Road to the West End then round Rutland Square so that she was off the main traffic route. Only took twenty minutes and she chastised herself for not going on foot more frequently. She pressed the bell for deliveries and the warden answered the intercom, clearly flummoxed to hear Viv's voice, since there was no car to alert her.

The door clicked open and Viv stepped into the foyer.

The warden waddled towards her, tight lipped and officious.

Viv didn't give her any preamble, just said, 'I'd like to see the CCTV footage for yesterday and the day before.' No explanation, just a request.

'Oh, I can't give you access to that. It would have to be cleared by . . .'

Viv put the flat of her hand up. 'Now, my mum has had a threatening encounter and I, as her immediate family, have a right to look at . . .'

It was the warden's turn to interrupt. 'I don't have the authority to do that.'

'Perhaps not, but with one phone call, which we are just about to . . .'

She took out her phone and glared at the warden in expectation of her giving up a number. She was not compliant but made a gesture for Viv to follow her to the office. Once there she rummaged through papers and drawers until she realised that Viv was going nowhere, and pressed a single digit on the landline on her desk.

Viv sighed and reminded herself that when people revelled in tiny victories it indicated their actual insecurity. But that didn't justify inappropriate behaviour. You just had to look at the legacy of Hitler or Stalin to witness what insecure people were capable of. Viv was convinced that her mum was unhappy with the way she was treated by this woman but she had too little proof. Once or twice recently when Viv had said she'd 'get the warden onto it' her mum had made excuses so that Viv wouldn't take action. Viv's mum was no shrinking violet yet this warden had some sort of power over her. Viv glanced round the small tidy room. A box of tissues disguised under a satin and lace cover crouched on the window sill, a bookcase with a few 'how to' books sat beneath a framed certificate on the wall stating that the woman had 'attended' a course on communication with the elderly. The warden caught her reading it and glared. The place smelled of mock lavender, definitely more chemical than organic and barely masking another stale smell, which Viv recognised as over-full vacuum cleaner.

The call took two minutes. The warden conceded and turned her computer screen round so that Viv could view it. A few clicks later she watched the film that Mand had talked about. There definitely was a man going directly up a ladder to her mum's first floor windows. Why would he do that if he was there to do the whole building? Surely he'd start at the top and work down? She stared at the paltry attempt he'd made at cleaning the window. There was more looking in than cleaning. What was he up to? Viv zoomed in to look for a logo on his clothing but she couldn't see anything. The company that the housing association employed had to wear uniforms.

The warden said, 'He's definitely not one of the usual men. They're all vetted and I haven't seen him before. Also, they're not allowed to work without uniforms and ID cards.' There was a knock at the office door. A resident wanted help to open the clothes drier. Reluctantly the warden went with the woman, which left Viv free to download the footage onto a USB stick. It was possible that she'd find the man on another database but not one that she would access easily from a public network computer.

She left the office without saying goodbye and nipped upstairs to her mum's flat. There was no answer when she knocked. She went back downstairs to the public rooms and through a window in the top of the door she saw her mum with a group of men and women concentrating on a watercolour class. Best leave her to it. She jogged home.

Chapter Two

Viv scraped the mould off a block of cheddar and put slivers of the remains on top of oatcakes. She bit into the first one and spat it out. Mouldy cheese was one thing but soft oatcakes, no way. Coffee with sugar would keep her going.

There wasn't much time before she had to pick up Sal and take her to the airport. A strange sensation began to curdle in her stomach. Better find a distraction. The new software she'd recently installed would help in the task she was about to begin. People were visible. It wasn't only China who had sophisticated surveillance. There were cameras and tech all around us gathering data to be used or stored in the event that someone or something needed to be traced. She believed that even the cameras used to deter speeding on motorways were constantly collecting data: registration numbers, the frequency of travel, the times of travel, and more importantly facial recognition of drivers. Big brother was much bigger and more far reaching than he'd ever been, but where there was information there was a desire to access it either by legal, or in her case not so legal means. She wasn't doing any harm just taking a peek. So she entered her new office space, a small cupboard built into the eaves of her flat. With no window to distract her, she had placed a large desk directly against a wall and bought three large monitors each with a different operating system. She closed the door behind her and settled down. In the safety of her tech-womb she toured cyberspaces that most people would never believe existed, never mind believe that she could access them. The film that she'd acquired from the warden was, as most of them were, grainy, but that wasn't difficult to remedy. Before installing her new software she'd have had to rely on Mac, or sneaking behind the firewall of the NTF services. She smiled. Her own super software was working a treat. The man who'd pretended to be her mum's window cleaner had a unique, not to mention convenient, identifying scar above his right eye but even without that she'd have been able to identify him. She ran his face through another system and soon found a name and his police record. He was a petty criminal, with a long history of theft, shoplifting, breaking and entering, mainly small retailers. She snorted. He'd been done once for nicking dozens of boxes of bubbly off a lorry before they'd made it to the supermarket. Nothing sophisticated, but from what she could make out he always had intelligence in advance. Possible connections to a gang or syndicate? No violence recorded didn't mean he hadn't used it, just that he hadn't been caught. Criminals were bright, creative people not to be underestimated. She'd known a few who'd given themselves up for a petty crime in the interest of something much greater going undiscovered. Her speculations helped to create a clearer picture, not always a bad thing. She laughed when people claimed, 'What you see is what you get.' Total BS. People were rarely what they let you see. Mostly they were the sum of what they were hiding. Freud was no slouch. She shifted in her chair and cracked her neck; she'd found out enough to dig in other avenues but now it was time to face the music with Sal.

Sal had convinced herself that a sabbatical in the USA was exactly what her career needed and that New York wasn't that far away. Besides, there were direct flights now from Edinburgh, so no excuses not to see each other. But the fact that Sal was going at all was the problem. Or was it her solution? They'd had the 'living together' chat and it hadn't ended well. The next thing that Viv knew Sal had applied and been accepted to do a year's exchange to NYU. Viv wasn't at all keen on the idea but preferred it to the live-in situation that Sal was pushing for. What was wrong with her? She didn't want to be with anyone other than Sal. That much she'd worked out after seeing Sal with someone else. A feeling of dread haunted her. The thought of not having Sal's company daily caused her gut to clench. Added to this emotional broth was the fact that she hated goodbyes. It took a certain kind of maturity to handle them and she wasn't there yet.

She arrived at Sal's tiny lower flat in the Stockbridge colonies and hovered at the gate to a postage-stamp-sized lawn reserved entirely for a Mollie the Collie emergency. It was a joke to call the space a garden, since garden presupposed a place to take pleasure in. Not so here – a wood store and two bins inhabited the single line of four paving slabs where previous residents might have parked a deck chair. Since there was no bark of acknowledgement, she assumed that Sal had arranged for Moll to stay with Brian up in Doune. Sal swung back the door before Viv had the chance to knock. No surprise there, since Sal was efficient and no doubt watching for Viv's arrival from the window.

'Ready?' Viv asked, not feeling in the slightest bit ready herself.

Sal nodded, 'Can you give me a hand with this?'

She stepped aside to reveal a huge bright yellow suitcase that could be seen from the moon. Viv grabbed hold of its handle and pulled it out onto the path. Viv waited at the gate while Sal retreated inside closing shutters and tending to whatever locking up and switching off had to be done before a long trip abroad. Viv swallowed hard as she pictured Sal meeting a whole department of new colleagues. Would she come back? Would she get sucked in by the American dream? Was there still such a thing? She hoped not.

Sal stepped out and closed the door, locked it with three different keys then remembered something else to do. Viv trundled the monster suitcase behind her towards the Rav, illegally parked on Glenogle Road. The Stockbridge Colonies was one of the most desirable areas of the city. Only a stone's throw from good pubs, shops and eateries, but the most enviable thing was the Victorian swimming baths right on the door step. She heaved the case into the back of the car and turned to watch Sal trying to organise another three bags. A rucksack kept slipping off her shoulder onto another bag looped over her arm. Another small but smart looking rucksack wouldn't stay on her other shoulder. How would she manage them all at the other end?

'What the hell are you carrying all that for?'

Sal shot her a don't-even-go-there glare as she stopped again to rearrange the ensemble.

Viv travelled lightly in the knowledge that people all over the world wore tee shirts and pants and brushed their teeth. No matter where she went she could purchase anything that she'd need, and if she couldn't nobody died. She took hold of the heaviest rucksack and strode to the Rav where she'd left the tailgate open. Sal threw the remaining bags in and jumped into the passenger side. They drove off in silence. Viv felt sick. She swallowed and tried to slow her breath. 'When's your first trip home?' It was out before she realised.

Sal snapped. 'God Viv, I've not even left yet.'

Viv bit back a jibe, and kept her eyes on the road. She chewed her lip as they drove round the back of the Botanic Gardens.

Sal said, 'I'm sorry. I didn't mean . . .' Silent tears rolled down her cheeks. She swiped them with the back of her hand then fumbled about in a pocket for a handkerchief. 'I knew this was a bad idea . . . I've forgotten tissues.'

Viv, relieved that she'd managed to contain her tears, pointed to the glove compartment. 'There's a box in there. Help yourself.'

Everyone has different ways of dealing with tension in relationships. These two wanted to be together for the long term, but Viv had this giant obstacle about living together. Sal wasn't a quitter, but at some level thought that a bit of distance might be a good thing, otherwise she wouldn't be on her way to the USA. She was clear about what she wanted. But after Dawn, Viv was scared and Sal knew it. Having an ex who'd treated her like an out of date fashion accessory meant Viv's defences were impenetrable. She'd given Dawn her heart and soul then been spat out like stale chewing gum. She could never let that happen again. It didn't seem to matter that she knew Sal was completely different; once bitten and all that.

Sal glanced across at her. 'I am sorry. I mean now isn't the time to be bitter. We are still together.' This sounded like a question.

Viv snorted, 'Yeah, with a large body of water between us.'

'I'll be home every couple of months. It's not as if they've given me a green card or anything. There's no chance of it becoming permanent. You do know that, don't you?'

'You doth protest too much methinks.' Viv kept her eyes firmly on the road ahead. Why would she mention a 'green card'?

Sal drew in a deep breath. 'We've been over this. You know it's an exchange sabbatical. One year. The prof from NYU won't want to spend the rest of her life at Central.'

Viv interrupted her. 'That's an odd way to think of it. It doesn't matter what she wants. It matters what you want. It matters how tied up in the American dream of profiling you become. No point in hypothesising about what some professor that you've never met might or might not want.' Her tone had risen out of her comfort zone. She told herself to quit while she was ahead. This was not the way to say goodbye.

Sal blew her nose. Viv admired the volume produced by such a petite woman. She welled up again. The driver of the car in front delayed his reaction to the traffic lights and Viv hit the horn. He threw her a rude gesture then stalled.

'For fuck sake!'

Sal stretched across and put her hand over Viv's. 'It's okay. We'll get there.'

An ambiguous statement when so much was at stake. How possible was it to sustain a relationship over such a distance? The whole idea of them having two roofs in Edinburgh drove Sal to distraction. They both knew that they could live on their own happily enough and Sal had suggested she'd like lots of weekends in the country which meant space was available if and when they needed it. Viv could take or leave the countryside but understood that Sal wanted a grown-up relationship, the kind where she came home in the evening and discussed her day over a glass of wine and a bowl of pasta, put her feet up and watched a bit of TV before going to bed with the person she loved. But understanding this, and at times even being drawn to the idea, it was still a step too far.

And now Sal was on her way to a new university with the FBI's new forensic profiling library and new colleagues. Way too much temptation. Viv's insides flipped. The slip-road to the airport was nose-to-tail with traffic and they sat in silence as the queue inched forward. It was as if they were being taunted by an external force, compelling them to confront whatever needed confronting – and yet they each shifted in their seats in silence. Their silence wasn't nothing; it was the weight of a particular something that sat like Sisyphus's rock between them. Neither believed in letting things lie, so before they reached the terminal Viv exhaled a long, loaded sigh. She couldn't pinpoint exactly what she felt but it was somewhere between frustration, exasperation and bloody mindedness. How could two women, known for their exceptional communication skills, not address what might happen next?

The traffic began to move enough for Viv to change up into third gear. It was agony. 'I suppose we have to just suck it and see.'

Sal turned to face her. 'Oookay. Odd choice of analogy though.'

They pulled into a space in the short-term car park and Viv jumped out and went to fetch a trolley. The sooner the inevitable was over the better. She returned, hauled Sal's giant case from the boot, and lifted it onto the trolley. Sal stood rooted to the spot swiping tears from her cheeks. Viv abandoned the bags and scooped Sal up into a tight embrace and spoke into her hair. 'We'll be fine. Just don't forget about me.'

Sal withdrew. 'How could you even say that?'

'Coz I don't know what else to say. We both know that you wouldn't be doing this if it wasn't for me.'

'Don't flatter yourself. I'm dying to get into this new job.'

'That, I suppose, is what I'm scared of. I'm scared that you'll love it and not come back.'

Sal stroked Viv's cheek. 'Now who's being daft? Of course I'm coming back. What would Moll do without me?'

The mention of Mollie had them both clinging to each other. Sal probably found it as difficult to leave the dog behind as she did Viv, but it didn't feel like that now. An airport security announcement brought them both back to the practicalities of getting Sal checked in and through to departures. With her arm around Sal's shoulder Viv wheeled the trolley towards the departures entrance. No mean feat with so many people bustling about and bollards to negotiate.

The queue for Sal's flight was snaking round its cordons. People, like the walking dead, slowly pushed their bags forward.

Suddenly Sal said, 'What am I doing?'

Viv looked at Sal to see if she'd changed her mind. But Sal was digging around in her rucksack.

She pulled out her ticket and flapped it in front of Viv, 'Business class. They paid for business class. We're in the wrong queue. Over there.' She pointed to a desk where a woman sat idle. 'That's where we should be.'

There were lots of people behind them now and they had a problem getting beneath the cordon to access the other desk. Only then did the penny drop and Viv realised how prestigious the post was that Sal was going to. She was being totally selfish by not embracing this as a big deal for Sal. She should be excited for her, not behaving like a spoiled child.

'Look Sal, this is a great chance for you. I could come and visit.'

Sal's look of alarmed disbelief confirmed just how badly behaved she'd been.

Viv rubbed her hands over her face, 'No, really. How smart are you getting to fly business class? No cattle in sight for you.'

Sal handed her ticket to the woman and turned to Viv. 'Nice that you're getting the hang of it.' She smiled and turned back to answer security questions about her luggage. Viv hovered and warmed to the idea of joining Sal in New York. A vision of a loft apartment with bare brick walls and endless space began to take shape.

'Send me pics of your accommodation.'

Sal nodded, still distracted by the process of her luggage being checked straight through to New York even though she was going to be at Heathrow for a couple of hours before the transatlantic hop.

'I'd have to fly cattle from Edinburgh direct.'

Sal didn't make eye contact. Viv needed to go through the necessary thought process in her own time.

'Yeah. I think that's doable. If you've got the space.'

Sal hooked her arm into Viv's, 'Oh, I think if I was sleeping in a hermit's cell I'd make space for you.'

By the time they stepped onto the escalator there were smiles on both of their faces.

Chapter Three

The drive home was a whole lot easier and Viv's shoulders were returning to their rightful position. In her head she planned when she could shift her clients to take time off. No point in going all that way just for the weekend.

Before she got back to the flat she received a text from Mac, 'Dinner at B's?'

She didn't answer until she was on her way upstairs. She sent a question back. 'Why? What are you up to?'

'Nothing. Just wanted to run something by you.'

'Nothing' was always something with Mac. She put the kettle on and checked her emails before answering. 'Okay. I've got stuff to do, so not late.'

The stuff she had to do could be done at any time, but it was best done while she was fresh, and that no longer applied in the middle of the night.

Mac replied, '7pm?'

She agreed, glancing at the time; only an hour to go. She was starving but knew if she went down the chocolate digestive route she'd take the edge off Bella's delicious dish of the day. She went back into her cubbyhole study and ran through more info on the petty thief. Nothing like trawling the net to lose track of time. Next time she looked up it was time to be at Bella's.

'Hi,' she said, panting after her sprint to the bistro.

Mac stood and pulled out the chair opposite him. Old manners were so seductive. 'She's got your fav on.' He nodded to the specials board. 'Venison casserole. Good weather for a hearty stew.'

She laughed, 'What the heck are you on? You sound like a TV chef.'

Bella arrived with menus but they both opted for the special and their usual beers.

Viv smiled, 'How's it going, Bella?'

'Not too bad. Apart from this Baltic weather. It keeps people in their sitting rooms bonding with the remote control.'

Viv laughed. An image of her mum popped into her head.

Mac said, 'Our gain. No need to give us small portions.'

Bella snorted, 'You've never had a small portion from me yet.'

Viv interrupted, 'No he hasn't but I have. Gender biased portions Bella, not PC.'

Bella shook her head and wandered off with their order.

'So what do you really want?'

Mac grinned, 'No point in bull shitting you is there?'

She shook her head, 'Nope.'

'It's unofficial.'

She interrupted him, 'When is it ever anything else with you guys?'

'You remember the sweep of the cyber analyst's consoles that you did?'

'Yes. It wasn't that long ago.'

'Well, we have another console that we'd like checked.'

Bella arrived with a basket of sourdough bread and a small bowl of pale yellow Italian butter. They tucked in without hesitation, confident that everything Bella served was tip-top.

'Oh, I could live on this.' Viv held up a slice of bread slathered with butter.

Bella called over her shoulder, 'Luckily you don't have to. There's more food on its way.'

'So, this console, who does it belong to?'

'Ah, well that's the thing.'

Viv leaned in, 'Top brass got found out at last?'

Mac leaned back. 'Was that a guess?'

She laughed, 'Kind of. But when you want me on board it's always a job that no one in-house would or should touch. So how high does it go?'

He raised his eyebrows, swallowed, then wiped his mouth with a napkin.

'Oh, you know, the seat next to God.'

Bella appeared with two piping hot dishes of casserole with mash on the side. 'Take your time. The plates are blistering hot. Don't want health and safety on my case.'

It took them a few minutes to divvy out the mash but once they'd had their first taste and agreed its merits Viv said, 'Who has already seen the console?'

Mac hesitated. 'Well, Gordon, but . . .'

'I can imagine what Gordon's "but" is. I take it he didn't find what you thought he'd find?'

'No, he didn't. But I'm sure there's something more on there than he . . .'

'Was willing to say or just couldn't find?'

'I think he genuinely didn't find it. You on the other hand . . .'

'Gordon's lazy. Or scared. Which do you think it is?'

'Not sure. That's why I think you'd dig a bit deeper. You're not scared or lazy.'

'Don't think seducing me with kind words will work.'

He pointed his fork at her, 'Ah, but it does. You are one sucker for kind words and especially today . . .'

He knew that Sal had left this afternoon.

'You're a mercenary sod. Using my emotional weakness to . . . get me to work for you.'

'So was that a yes?'

She finished a mouthful and nodded, 'Sure. Information is currency. The more data I have the more swollen my virtual account gets.'

'I knew you'd be fascinated. Unlike most folk you'd never be seduced by dosh. It's always about the knowledge.'

'Knowledge has always been more valuable than money, but I don't need to tell you that.'

They continued eating in relative silence, each of them making Neanderthal noises of appreciation.

Finally, Bella cleared the table, and said, 'I've got vanilla pannetone. Interested?'

Viv said, 'Is the Pope a Catholic?'

'I think the current one is.'

Mac held up his finger. 'I'm in.'

'Coffees?'

'The usual,' Mac said, without asking Viv.

She said, 'So when do you want me to take a look?'

He shifted in his seat.

She laughed, 'You guys are always chasing your tail. I take it you need it yesterday?'

He sighed, 'So can you come to Fettes with me after this?'

'God, Mac, you're such a charmer. A girl could get ideas.'

'Maybe, but not a girl like you. Are you in or not?'

'Sure am.'

They finished dinner and Mac went to pick up the bill. She beat him to it and scooped it up. No you don't. Fifty fifty. You'll get my invoice all in good time.'

'I was being friendly.'

'No such thing as a free lunch, or dinner. God, I hardly remember which meal I've just eaten I was so hangry.'

As they reached the street Mac said, 'So how was it with Sal?'

'Oh, as you'd expect.' Now wasn't the time for her to revisit her heart. 'I'll take my own car in case you decide you're doing an all-nighter.'

The car park at Fettes was quiet, but that was no surprise since it was no longer HQ for the whole of Lothian and Borders. She waved to the duty sergeant on reception, but Mac bypassed the formal signing in process and rapidly led her to the floor below, as if he didn't want people to see her.

'This is clandestine.'

'I've had permission to get you in "with as little disturbance as possible". The powers that be don't want feathers ruffled.'

'You mean beyond the ones that have been already?'

Mac used his security card to access a room and the door hissed aside. 'The info we've got is enough to hang him, I mean metaphorically.'

'Yeah I got that, we've not been hanging for a while now.' She shook her head. 'Sometimes I think you've got no idea who I am. And by the way how come you still don't have iris recognition on that door? How long has it been?'

He shrugged. 'The door still opens with a card.'

She rummaged in her bag and pulled out three similar cards. 'Like these you mean.'

He tried to grab them. 'How did you get those?'

She jumped out of reach. 'Oh no you don't. I worked hard for these. Besides I'm not here under false pretences.'

'You wouldn't be here if I didn't know how valuable . . .'

'Piss off with the flattery and show me the console.'

Mac took her to the back of the room where a row of grey desks had been assembled to spread out an assortment of evidence. Sheets of printed pages in clear bags, a rubber, pencil, and pens each in its own bag. She stretched out to lift one.

'Best not to touch. You never know when your prints will be used against you.' He pulled out two pairs of latex gloves. 'Here.'

The many layers of suspicion within the service were as sticky as a stack of pancakes with maple syrup.

'Is this what you want me to look at?' She pointed at a screen.

He nodded and rolled a chair across from another console. She sat and began tapping on the keyboard.

He rolled another chair over. 'You won't be able to get in without the pass . . .'

'Oh paleeeze.'

He hovered as she continued to tap and the screen went black before suddenly becoming covered in thousands of characters. She scrolled and scrolled until she spotted something. 'See that?' She pointed to the screen. 'You want me to explore that. I think Gordon was scared and if I was in house I'd probably have done the same. I mean lied. There's no way that he didn't spot that.'

'Why do you say that?'

'Because that row of numbers on the end means . . .'

Mac glanced around as if there was someone else in the room. There wasn't.

She said, 'What? There's always someone listening. I'm surprised you don't all have a corn plaster over your cameras and cotton wool over the mics. Simple solutions.'

'So what exactly does that mean?'

'It means communication with an outside source.'

'Outside where?'

'If I said go to Europe and travel east.'

'We thought that was it but we couldn't be absolutely sure. Is there only one entry?'

'So far, but that one entry takes you off this server. Shall we take a look?'

He glanced around him again. 'I'm nervous of . . .'

She laughed, 'You don't say. I'll send you this Url and you can decide if it's enough and if not you can take a look at the other stuff. Got a spare USB stick?'

He handed her one. 'No, just do it. We're running out of time.'

She stared at him, 'I take it the "we" you mean isn't us?' She pointed to herself then back to him.

'No, you're right. It's bigger than the two in the room.'

'How big?'

'Pretty big.'

She continued to search and download information. 'You shouldn't ever ask your in-house guys to do this kind of stuff. They just feel trapped between a rock and a hard place. I mean if they find something, it means they weren't vigilant the first time round. Also, if whoever this console belongs to gets off, they've got some poor cyber analyst to come after. Either way it has to be someone neutral-ish.' She grinned, 'Like me.'

'No one is neutral.'

'No, they are not, but I'm not worried about losing my nine to five. Oh and another thing, once you're ahead in this game you have to keep at it and I'm not sure your guys do. Too easy to become complacent when you know there's a pension coming. Me, well, I'm just a hungry, nosey sod. Here,' she handed him the USB. 'Now that does contain enough to hang them.'

'You make it look so simple, but it's not.'

'It is simple once your eyes have been trained to spot anomalies. It's like a wallpaper pattern. If you stare at it you see all sorts of shapes repeating but if one of those rolls hasn't been hung straight and you get an overlap or a kink, you can't unnotice it. Just like that on a page of encrypted info.'

He shook his head. 'I appreciate you're trying to give me the idiot's guide but there's more to it.'

She shrugged, 'Have it your own way, babe. You usually do. Now if we're done entrapping your colleague I've got other work to do.' She put her hand on his arm. 'Hope it works out. I'm confident you're on the side of the angels.'

She walked to the door and put one of her cards up to the sensor; it hissed open. Mac rubbed his hands over his face. 'You are the limit. But thanks, I really do appreciate your help.'

'Invoice will arrive in your inbox before you can say . . .'

He interrupted her, 'Actually . . .'

She got the message, 'Okay, cash invoice next time we meet?'

He nodded and held up the USB. 'This is the icing on the cake if we need it. Hopefully he'll go voluntarily without any noise. We'll see.'

Chapter Four

Thursday

Viv huffed and puffed as she scrapped a thick layer of ice off the Rav's windscreen. Not the start she needed on a busy hair morning. She'd forgotten her gloves and had to blow warmth back into her hands. Nothing worse than a cold car – apart from all the things that were worse. It took ten minutes to drive down through the Canongate and round the back of Abbey Hill to reach Jinty's house on Regent's Terrace. She hadn't heard back from her and wasn't feeling inspired by the idea of fitting in a new head of hair. Once she'd parked and put a ticket inside the car she grabbed her kit from the boot and walked over an expanse of cobbled road to the grand Georgian townhouse. She rang the bell, listening to it peal through the cavernous hallway while appreciating her distorted image in a highly polished, brass lion's-head knocker.

She stamped her feet on a giant coir mat to prevent her toes from freezing up. Jinty opened the door and said in a pitch that was even lower than usual, 'Hi Viv, soooo lovely to see you.' This was normal, but the look on her face didn't match her words, and she was shaking her head with her eyebrows knitting together. No mean feat. Viv tried to work out what the message was as Jinty took hold of her sleeve and guided her in.

Jinty whispered, 'I've told him you are too busy to do it.'

Confused, Viv said, 'Did you get my email?'

Jinty nodded furiously, 'Yes.' Then raising her voice. 'That's no problem. We completely understand. He'll look fine. It just needs a good wash and blow dry and I'll help with that before he leaves.'

Jinty swept upstairs with her forefinger to her lips and beckoned Viv to follow. Once inside Jinty's bedroom with the door closed firmly behind them Jinty dropped her shoulders and said, 'He's too weird. Too weird.' She pointed to the room below indicating where he was. 'I'm convinced he has an ulterior motive for meeting you. At first I could see what he meant about his hair but then he said something that didn't make sense. As if seeing you was part of a plan. He doesn't make eye contact and he's been too inquisitive about your life. I mean you are a very interesting woman, no one believes that more than me, but why would he want to know about a hairdresser in a city that he's never been in before. Tell me that's not odd.'

This certainly grabbed Viv's attention. 'Why would he do that? I don't know any composers and where was it you said he was from?'

'He's from Berlin.'

'No, I definitely don't know anyone from Berlin.' She thought of Ronnie and his Wagnerian description of her visitor. 'What does he look like?'

'Oh, he's a handsome devil, but there's something not quite right about him, and I'm not sharing you with anyone who doesn't deserve you. Now let's get this,' she held a few strands of her hair aloft, 'sorted. I have to look half decent for the concert.'

'Okay. But is he tall and blond and handsome?'

'Yes, he is. Was that a guess?'

'You don't happen to have a photograph of him, do you?'

'Sure. I have a flyer for the concert. I don't care how famous he is; he doesn't deserve you . . . I'm surprised you haven't heard of him. His name is Kurt Hahn. I'll get that flyer for you.' She moved towards the door.

'No. Let's get it when I'm on my way out.'

Jinty looked concerned, 'Why do you want to see him?'

'It could be nothing, but I've had a visitor to my flat. I wasn't there, but my neighbour told me that there'd been a tall blond man at the door. You know me, not one for coincidences.'

'Why on earth would he come to your flat? And how would he know where you live?'

'Good questions.'

Viv set up her hairdressing kit and made a start on Jinty's hair. She was one of Viv's best adverts. She even looked glamorous when she was gardening. The cut was easy but the blow-dry would have to survive a tsunami. Jinty was an Edinburgh society hostess, whose parties were the talk of the town. Viv had had so many people who'd tried to ingratiate themselves with Jinty via her; anything to wangle an invitation. Viv did everything possible to avoid them.

Once she'd switched the drier off they continued their conversation. Not that the drier usually stopped them but because he was somewhere in the house it seemed prudent to keep their voices down, impossible over 2,000 revs a minute.

Jinty said, 'I had thought of having a few people in to celebrate, but I'm glad that I didn't. He's leaving early tomorrow, thank goodness. When will I ever learn? People ask me to do them favours and you know how difficult it is to say no.'

'So, you don't really know him?'

'No. Never set my eyes on him before. Just got an email from a London friend begging me to put up this wonderfully talented, rising star . . . he's terribly abrupt . . . and why would he seek you out?'

Viv racked her brain for anyone that she might have bumped into and not remembered but shook her head – she wasn't the type to let a tall handsome German slip her mind. Once Jinty's hair was sprayed within an inch of its life they made their way back down stairs. Jinty slipped into the kitchen, leaving Viv in the hallway, then returned with the flyer. Just as she handed it to Viv a door adjacent to the kitchen, which Viv knew to be the snug, opened and Kurt Hahn stepped out, filling the space between the two women.

Jinty, a consummate diplomat, said, 'Ah, Kurt, this is Vivian Fraser.'

He offered Viv his hand and they shook briefly, 'Very good to meet you, Miss Fraser.'

Jinty said, 'Oh, it's Doctor, actually.'

A look of confusion crossed his face but he recovered, 'Apologies. Doctor Fraser.' Formal. Too formal, with a nervous tic under his right eye.

'No need, everyone calls me Viv.'

He made a slight gesture with his head to one side as if he was expecting her to continue, but she was silent.

Jinty said, 'Viv's terribly busy.' And she hustled her towards the door. 'Speak soon,' was all she said as she ushered Viv out onto the front steps, obviously in a flap.

As Viv walked over the road towards the Rav she heard Jinty squeal and come running after her, 'I forgot to pay you. Here. Let's have coffee. I'll ring you.' She handed Viv a cheque, rubbed her forearm and bounded back inside. The whole experience was totally surreal. Ronnie was right; he was handsome, but what the devil could he want with her? She started up the Rav's engine and looked at the flyer. She'd check with Ronnie that it was the same guy. She already knew the answer to that, but best be sure.

It was unlike Jinty not to have coffee on the go and now Viv was slipping into caffeine deprivation. She started the Rav and glanced back at the house, wondering if Jinty was scared. She was a good judge of character, you can't entertain so many people and not become an anthropologist, but her performance today was off. Viv's phone vibrated. An incoming text from Sal read, 'Arrived in snowstorm. Landed after third attempt' with a tearful emoji. Oh God, Sal hated flying and was particularly terrified of landings. Thank God she was safe now.

Viv's next client, an archivist at the National Library, had her hair cut during her lunch break, down in one of the miles and miles of stacks. Illicit visits to the nooks and crannies, places the public would never see, was a perk of Viv's job. She'd been doing this one for a couple of years. In the same tiny spot surrounded by narrow corridors with floor to ceiling shelves of ancient boxed documents. Miles of knowledge stored underground made her palms damp with anticipation. She'd spent many a long day upstairs in the National's special collections department wearing white cotton gloves, reading first edition books on Freud. She imagined some poor sod walking and walking these stacks then having to climb a ladder in search of an obscure tome. There had been times when she'd waited half an hour, more, for a book to be delivered to her. She reminded herself to pay more attention to what was actually in the stacks where she'd be cutting hair today.

Melanie, a small elfin-faced woman, with a habit of changing her hair colour as regularly as her socks, pushed open the emergency door of the basement, the staff access from the Cowgate, and ushered Viv into their usual space, barely two metres square. Today Melanie's hair was pale blue. Her outfit an array of clashing reds and violets finished with a pair of rainbow DMs. Viv quickly laid out her sheet on the floor and positioned a folding chair that Melanie brought out from a cupboard where stationery was stored. Melanie was tetchy, which was nothing new; she was always concerned that they'd be caught by her boss. Viv wasn't sure what the result of being caught would be, but she didn't imagine it would incur quite the wrath that Melanie thought it would. The process only took twenty minutes, with Melanie dismissing the idea of a blow dry as too noisy, and terrified that hot air might set off the sensitive alarm system, in place for the security of the manuscripts. As Melanie rummaged around in her huge tapestry bag for money to pay, Viv scanned the shelves for catalogue identification marks on boxes. If she could remember what the first few letters were, she'd be able to go into the online catalogue and find out what the boxes contained. Appalled that she hadn't asked about their contents until now she said, 'Don't you ever tire of running these corridors for other people?'

Melanie's forehead creased. 'I don't know what you mean. I love my job. I love that all this knowledge is available to anyone – anyone who wants access to it. It's one of the greatest collections that exists and it's growing every day.'

Viv, infected by Melanie's passion, said, 'So what's in these?' She patted the shelf nearest to her and immediately released the musty smell of old paper.

Melanie stepped forward and glanced at the identifying tape on the front of the box. 'These contain estate maps. Not terribly interesting unless you're into old houses that were requisitioned during the Second World War.'

Viv was not particularly interested, but she knew a woman who would be. Sal's place in the country had been requisitioned. Sal had pointed out a row of old, now disused, telegraph poles that had been erected on the estate by the army. Melanie was right, this vast library was evidence of the democratisation of knowledge. Joe Blogs could walk in the front door, get himself a reader's ticket and access anything in the archives. Amazing.

As she was leaving Melanie said, 'Would you like a proper tour?'

It hadn't occurred to Viv that that would be possible but she said, 'I'd love one. When?'

'I can arrange it with my boss. I'll email you with some dates. It'll take a couple of hours. So best do it at the end of a working day.'

'Great. Look forward to that.'

Once an academic always an academic. Anything to do with books and knowledge got her fired up. At times like this she regretted not taking a full-time teaching post, but she had had her hair clients to think about. They'd stuck with her through thick and thin and she hadn't wanted to let them down. Besides she was as addicted to cutting their hair as they were to having her cut it. A full-time lectureship may have made life simpler but simple had never been her thing.

Her next client was in the Grassmarket, an antique dealer with a passion for miniature portraits. What new acquisitions might he have today? She pushed her hair back from her eyes and smiled. He was always going to find an undiscovered Rembrandt but so far, no luck. She pressed the buzzer for his flat. No answer. She pressed again. Still no answer. She took out her phone and rang his number. It went straight to voicemail. She left a message then wandered back towards her own flat, stopping to have a look at the knitwear in the window of Bill Baber's.

Chapter Five

As she approached her building she was surprised to see Mand with one foot hovering on the step outside the front door.

'Is everything all right?' Her first thought was that something had happened to their mum.

Mand, dressed in cream skinny jeans, a cream down jacket and cream ankle boots, pushed off the step to make space for Viv to open up, and shrugged, 'I'm not sure.' She tucked an imaginary hair behind her ear with beautifully manicured, pale pink nails.

'What do you mean you're not sure? Mum's either all right or she's not.'

'I think mum's okay but . . . let's go inside.'

Viv unlocked the door and they made their way up to Viv's flat. It was the first time that Mand had visited and Viv hoped she'd left it in a fit state. Mand's house was an immaculate minimalist space where little evidence of life was to be found outside of a cupboard door. James, Viv's nephew, would no sooner stop playing with a toy than it was picked up and put back in its rightful place. White carpets and shiny objets d'art were not the ideal play things for a toddler and yet Mand didn't seem able to give them up. Mand stepped over the threshold and looked around but said nothing. Nothing in words. Viv dropped her rucksack in the hall and went straight into the kitchen to put the kettle on.

'Coffee?'

Mand followed, 'How long have you been here now?'

'Couple of years. Not counting. But what's up? It's not like you to venture over to the dark side.'

Mand bristled. She was every bit the New Town woman, preferring wide streets and invisible neighbours. The Old Town was crammed with people coming and going, pubs spilling over and restaurants leaking the smells of exotic ingredients. Mand wouldn't live here if someone paid her to, but it was what Viv loved about it.

Mand said, 'I don't know if I'm overreacting.'

Viv couldn't stop herself from raising her eyebrows. Mand was the mistress of overreaction.

Mand continued, 'I've just been at mum's – James is at play group – and I found her going through that box of old photographs.'

Viv opened her eyes wide in mock surprise and turned her hand round and round for Mand to continue.

'Well, I went to the loo and when I went back into the sitting-room she was stashing a piece of paper back into a compartment in the box that I didn't even know existed. A tiny edge of it was still visible, but she shut the box quickly as if she didn't want me to see it. I wonder if we should take a look at whatever it is? Also she's edgy. When I arrived the door was double locked. She never locks her door.'

'You do know that that could be a symptom of something else?'

Mand sighed, 'You got that wrong last time, and I don't believe it this time. She's spooked by something.'

They had a running argument about whether their mum had the beginnings of dementia. The last time it had come up Mand had taken her to see the GP, but it turned out that her confusion was caused by a UTI and there was nothing wrong with her cognitive ability. Viv conceded that she'd got it wrong, but it didn't mean that was the case now.

Viv said, 'What do you want me to do?'

'Well, one of us has to take a look.'

Viv handed Mand a cup of black coffee and they went down the hall to the sitting-room.

Mand glanced around and crossed to the window. Viv loved the view and waited to hear Mand's reaction.

'Nice view. Noisy though.'

Viv smiled, 'Yeah it is. Comforting.'

Mand said, 'Well, will you take a look or shall I? I don't want you to think I'm snooping for no reason.'

This was the best side of Mand. She was honest to her core.

She sat on the edge of the ottoman and took in all of Viv's paintings and prints. 'D'you have help to clean this place?'

'No. I blitz it every now and then but you wouldn't want to eat your dinner off my floors any time soon.'

Mand shook her head. 'You think you've got me taped but you haven't. My OCD is what's kept me sane.'

Viv almost choked on her coffee at the irony. She knew what Mand meant, though. The ritual of perfect placement and tidying had its benefits and without that Mand would be even more uptight. Everyone found ways to survive and Viv wasn't immune from the odd moment of crazy realignment herself. Not so long ago, in Bella's bistro with Mac, one of the prints on the wall was sitting at an odd angle and the whole time that Mac was speaking she was distracted by it. Eventually he'd asked her what was wrong. She got up and adjusted the print, then gave him her full attention.

'Why don't we both do it?'

Mand looked surprised. 'Okay. When?'

Viv checked the time on her computer. 'We could go now, but she'll guess something's up.'

'She's out. A bus trip with the women from the . . . I saw the bus arrive.'

Neither of them knew what to call the place their mum lived in. It wasn't a care home and it wasn't sheltered accommodation. It was a hybrid: independent living with a bit of help if you needed it. Viv had settled on 'the Pound', since it was the name for the home that cats and dogs were taken when they were unwanted. No nursing care in their mum's place though; that much they'd made explicit. If she was away on a day trip, now would be a good time to check out the box. Without another word they put their cups in the kitchen and headed out to the street.

'My car is over here.' Mand gestured to her Lexus on Victoria Street.

'How did you manage to get that? I rarely get a space close to . . .'

Mand grinned, 'So living here is not all good?'

'I don't think it'll kill me to walk a few metres to my car. But when I've got a bag of kit or groceries it's a drag, I'll give you that.'

They jumped into Mand's car and drove to Haymarket. The car smelled new, but only because it was valeted so regularly. Mand's ex was always looking for ways to win her back by dangling goodies, like the car, as carrots. The car was posh admittedly, but not exactly child friendly; then there was said valet service and some serious financial support, including private nursery. Viv had to give her sis credit for not taking him back, although she still enjoyed company perks that benefited James. None of this would have happened if Doug hadn't been discovered attempting to squirrel finances offshore. She glanced over at Mand, a good-looking woman who Viv guessed wouldn't be on her own forever.

Viv said, 'Did the warden go with them?'

'How would I know? I didn't see her earlier.'

'Fingers crossed she has, or, even better, she's gone to live with an ancient aunt in New Zealand.'

'Have you got a problem with her?'

'Yes. Why? Have you not? She drives me nuts with her officious smugness. She's unkind and mum's scared of her. Why would that be?'

'D'you think she's threatened her?'

'I don't know. But mum's never exactly been worried about speaking her mind until this new warden arrived. Now when I say we should speak to her about something, take the central heating for starters, mum won't let me. It is as if she is scared of upsetting her. Getting the heating sorted is the warden's job. So now mum lives in a bikini state.'

'I'd noticed it was warm, but hadn't thought that mum was uncomfortable.'

'Oh, she's not. She lives in a tee shirt and baggy linen trews. She doesn't even bother to put socks on.'

Mand went to push another imaginary stray hair off her face and mistakenly scratched her head dislodging another hair from its tight bun.

'You're right. Why didn't I notice that?'

'You've been distracted with James and it's probably suited you to have a warm environment for him.'

'Yeah, but not so warm as to have mum sitting in her summer clothes in the middle of winter.'

They pulled up on the opposite side of their mum's building to where Viv would have parked, a legal space at the back away from the peering eyes of the warden.

'Do you always park here?'

Mand nodded. 'I use the back door.' She dangled a set of keys.

Viv had keys somewhere but it wouldn't occur to her to go into her mum's home if she wasn't there. Although, happy to make an exception now.

The flat always seemed much smaller when the sisters were in it together. They sidled round each other in search of the box, a familiar item, because it had housed the family photograph collection since before they were born: a brown mock crocodile skin square box about eighteen inches by eighteen inches by eighteen inches. Not easy to conceal but their mum had managed to force it beneath her bed and cover it with a bag of crocheted blankets.

'Mand. Can you lift up the bed while I try and pull this out? How the hell she managed to get it under here is anyone's guess.'

'Here, let me help.'

With a bit of tugging Viv managed to free it, but a corner of it caught on the old bedsprings and ripped. 'Shit. We'll have to fix that before we put it back.'

'That the royal we?'

Viv shook her head. 'Let's see what's inside.'

Viv opened the box and riffled through the photographs. Seeing images of her dad tugged at her heart.

Mand said, 'Give it here. If you stop to look at every picture she'll be back and we won't have the paper.' Mand ran her hand round the inside of the box but couldn't feel anything suspect. She slid her manicured fingernails round the top and caught a fine invisible pocket, which she prised apart. 'There's no way we'd have found this when . . .'

Best not to finish a sentence that implied their mum's demise.

She pulled out the sheet of paper. Yellowed with age and with a stamp across the original address declaring it, 'Top Secret'.

Mand glanced at Viv. 'What the . . .'

'It must be something to do with dad.'

'But it's got mum's name on it, not dad's.'

Viv took the document and read what she could, since some of the words were blacked out. It didn't make sense. She handed it back to Mand and put her hand into the pouch inside the box. At the bottom she felt something else. She slipped out a receipt stapled to a small sepia photograph of a woman. Her hairstyle looked sixties, maybe early seventies. Their parents never had disposable income in their entire lives so what the heck was her mum doing with a receipt for £450,000? They sat on the floor of their mum's bedroom and tried to make sense of what they were handling.

'Why so secretive about this? Why keep it tucked away where no one, not even we could find it? I mean if you hadn't interrupted her . . . It's weird.' Viv took out her phone and was about to take a photograph when there was a light knock at the door.

Mand put her finger to her lips and shook her head. It was as if they were back in childhood caught doing something illicit by one of their parents. They both put a hand over their mouth; a rare glimpse of a past that they'd lost sight of. The person knocking shuffled by and they each let their breath go.

'Shit. D'you think you should take a photograph? She sure as hell doesn't want us to see any of this.' Mand ran her hand over the yellow document. The receipt wasn't that old. There was a date obscured by a crease where a corner had been folded over in storage. Viv took a few photographs with her phone and they tucked the papers back into the box.

Mand said, 'What will we do about that little tear? She'll notice it.'

'Only if she has reason to take it out again. We'll risk it. She'll notice if it's been mended as well. You know what she's like; never misses a trick.'

They nodded their agreement and Mand held up the bed as Viv pushed the box back under so as not to damage it any further. They left the same way they'd come in. Once back in the car Viv took out her phone and stared at the documents. Magnifying the receipt made it easier to see the date. It was only five years old. They drove back to the West Bow. Mand had to pick up James but they agreed to speak later. Viv took the stairs two at a time and spent the next couple of hours searching sites where there was a chance she'd find out who the woman in the photograph was. It was slow work and eventually, after being up too many blind alleys, she interrupted the search to answer the call of her belly rumbling in protest. She stumbled out of her new 'office', rubbed her eyes as if she'd surfaced from underground, and went in search of her phone.

There was a message from Mac reminding her about yoga; he must have been too distracted last night. He reminded her weekly and occasionally she went. She checked the time. If she got a bend on she'd make it. She drank a large glass of water to fill her up then jogged down the Grassmarket to Dance Base where she spotted Mac chatting to a woman at the entrance. She held back. The woman was fawning, throwing her head back and laughing too loudly at something he said. Mac shrank back when she touched his arm. Viv intervened.

'Hi, I got your message.'

Mac, visibly relieved, said, 'Great!' He greeted her with a hug and a kiss. 'This is Viv,' he said to the woman, whose face crumpled. She recovered enough to be polite, 'Hi. Nice to meet you. I'm Olivia.'

Mac said, 'Shall we?' and ushered Viv by the small of her back into the studio. Olivia's phone rang and she pointed to it. Mac waved and he and Viv continued to the class.

'So?'

'So what?'

'So what was that about?'

'I am forever in your debt. She comes to this class and one of the others and asks me each week if I'll join her for dinner. Running out of excuses. But now that you're here . . .'

Viv scratched her head. 'Not heard of the words: I'm not interested?'

'Who'd say that? It would be cruel. I've managed to get away with work commitments so far, but now you're here we can have dinner.'

'How d'you know I'm not committed?'

'I don't, but every time you've come to the class it's been because you wanted company to eat. Call me a detective if you like. '

She play punched him but he swerved out of reach.

'Told you! Dinner?'

'You bet. In fact we could skip the class and go straight to Bella's.'

'No chance. You have to earn your treats.'

'Don't even go there with the bubble gum psych.'

The teacher began the first stretches and Viv glared at Mac, who smirked then looked the other way.

Ashtanga was such a ferocious work-out that a shower was essential after it. On their way to the changing area she said, 'Really ought to shower.'

He threw her a towel, 'Here, use this.'

They met out front ten minutes later. No sign of Olivia.

Bella's was busy, but she cleared a table by the window and left them with menus and the specials board. Ravenous now, Viv wanted everything on the board.

'I'll have the same as last night.'

Mac said, 'Sounds good. I'll have the same.'

Bella returned and said, 'Lucky, that's the last of it.'

'Still got mash?'

Bella said, 'Still got some buttery mash.'

'Silly me.' Viv rubbed her hands together.

When she was this hungry she couldn't think straight. Bella brought them their usual beers and a basket of bread and they tucked in.

After a few bites Viv said, 'That's much better. So how useful was that info?'

He glared at her.

She batted her hand, 'Okay, let's not talk about that. So what's really going on with Olivia?'

He nodded as he finished a mouthful, 'Oh, she's a rescuer. Stalking me for weeks. But I'm fine; your timing couldn't have been better. Another woman around is perfect. She'll stop trying to save me now . . . but never mind that. I'm guessing you've got something on your mind.'

'No, I haven't.'

He pointed with his fork over the table, 'Exactly! No one is that defensive for nothing.'

'What do you mean defensive?' She couldn't help noticing the shrill sound that came out of her mouth.

'So what's up?'

Bella arrived with their mains. 'Right, I'll leave you two to it then.' She grinned. Bella had told Viv that eventually she and Mac would see what everyone around them had seen forever; that they should be an item. Viv wasn't completely averse to the idea, but somehow the timing had never been right. Either one or other was usually involved with someone else, although his record was pretty abysmal. Which was saying something next to Viv.

'By the way we must stop meeting like this. Folk'll talk. I mean more than they do already.' She grinned. 'I should have mentioned this last night but I've had time to do a bit more digging today and well . . . Let me run this by you. Yesterday I had a strange visitor. And so did my mum.'

'Okay. So that's two strange visitors or the same strange visitor to both? And what's strange about them?'

She hesitated. 'Different visitors to each. Strange, though. Both my mum and I have had visits but not in any traditional way. My guy came to visit when I was out.'

'He didn't get in surely?'

'No, he didn't get in, but Ronnie thought he heard him put something through my letterbox. He hadn't, so he must have been peering into the flat. So that's the first oddity. The second is that I think the guy is a famous composer pianist who is staying with a client of mine. He asked if I'd do his hair.'

Mac raised his eyebrows.

'Yeah right. It didn't happen, but I did meet him. I bumped into him when I was on my way out after doing this woman's hair.' She sniffed. 'I'm lucky my clients are pretty protective. She said he'd been asking too many questions about me, so she told him I was too busy to cut his hair. I've never met him before, but I wondered if I'd somehow rattled his cage inadvertently.'

'Interesting. And your mum?'

'My mum has her windows cleaned by the same man twice a year and a guy turned up unannounced, not claiming to be the window cleaner, just demonstrating it. He faffed about at her windows as if he was doing a recce, then took off. The usual guy has to do all of the windows in the Pound. This guy wasn't interested in anyone else.'

Mac laughed. 'You know you shouldn't call it that. One day . . .'

She held her hand up, 'I know, I know. Odd, though, to have two peeping toms in one week.'

They continued to munch through their food. 'Oh wow, this is so good.'

'So how're you doing now that Sal's gone?'

'Oh God, poor Sal. I realised at the airport what a complete arse I'd been. It's such a fantastic opportunity for her . . .'

'But you'll miss her.'

She nodded and avoided eye contact, 'Course I will. Just have to keep busy. And I'll go out to visit.'

'Really?'

'Yes, "really"! Why do you say it like that?'

He shook his head. 'No reason. But ok, what about this stranger, did you get a photograph of him?'

She raised her eyes. 'You think I'm a total amateur. Of course I got a photograph.' She dug into her pocket and handed over the flyer. 'He obviously doesn't look quite as good as that in real life. They've given him a good air brushing, but he is handsome in a Germanic kind of way.' She laughed. Ronnie was absolutely right in his description.

Mac stared at the flyer, 'Are you sensing a puzzle? Too many wee bits and pieces going on in a short time?'

'Oh, it gets better. Mand turned up at my flat.' She grinned as she watched it sink in. 'Yes, that's right, Mand, my sister, at my flat. I never thought I'd see the day. Anyway she pitched up concerned about our mum.'

'The window cleaner again?'

'No, well I'm not sure about that, but she'd seen my mum hiding something and couldn't work out why she would. Upshot is that we went to my mum's and found the paper she was hiding and it . . .' She took out her phone and scrolled until she found the image of the document and handed it to Mac. She loved the way that Mac's face told so many stories – surprise, amazement, intrigue, then a call to action sort of look. No poker wins for him.

'So this is fascinating. What do you know about your mum's past that might include her having dealings with the secret services?'

'Well, that's just it. I can't believe it. There was nothing about our childhood that would make me think she was involved with anything other than secretarial work. But when I think about it now I suppose that's exactly how she'd want it to look. If she was she must have been fantastic at her job. Should I just ask her outright?'

'You could, but she'll be old school. They took their Official Secrets Act way more seriously than today's spies.'

Viv snorted, 'Spy! She wasn't a spy.'

Mac raised his eyebrows, 'Naive or what? You think that that kind of letter was sent out to anyone?'

Viv shook her head, 'How weird is this? But there's more . . . hidden in the same compartment, she had this.' She scrolled through her phone again and handed it back to Mac with the photograph on the screen. 'No idea who she is, and check out the amount on that receipt. There's no way my mum or dad ever had money like that and yet there it is in black and white. Too weird.'

Mac said, 'You mentioned you'd done a bit of digging?'

She nodded. 'Of course. So far all I've got is the guy who's not a window cleaner but a petty thief. It seems odd that he's targeting my mum. Out of all the people living in the Pound she is the least likely to have dosh stashed away. So, I'm seeing a connection between the thief and these documents. Also, she had locked herself in. Why would she do that?' Viv stretched, then wiped her mouth with her napkin. 'There will be a connection, but I'm not sure what kind of a hornet's nest I'll be poking . . . Shit, imagine if she was, as you say, a spy.'

'I bet the more you mull over your childhood the more possible my hypothesis becomes. She'll have been on courses and you'll have stayed with your Grannie, or someone will have stayed with you, sleepovers with pals, anything to keep family life normal.'

'We did do sleepovers with pals, but it was rare for her to be away. I'm not saying it didn't happen; just can't remember it being a thing. My dad was always working, always working. I'll ask Mand. She has completely different memories to me. Between us we'll patch a picture together and if that fails I'll ask my mum.'

Mac said, 'The fact that you do what you do must have come from somewhere.' He stared at the photograph on her phone. He magnified it. 'Look.'

She leaned over. 'What?'

'See that curve? That's a Nissen hut. I don't think the photograph is as old as WW2. I could be wrong but most MOD facilities were supposed to be decommissioned soon after the war. Those that were left were used up until . . . wait, actually there are still a couple in existence now but they're not in military use.'

She screwed up her eyes, 'I wonder who took the photograph?'

He sighed, 'There's a question for your mum.'

She raised her eyebrows and said, 'Where are these camps? In fact let's see that photograph.' She enlarged it and saw what he meant. I remember seeing huts like that when we were children on our caravan holidays at Findhorn.'

He nodded. 'They're still there. I think only used as storage by the local farmer.'

'Coincidence?'

'What?'

'That we had holidays in a place with Nissen huts?'

'That might be pushing it but it's worth being curious about. Vis a vis your mum as a spy you've got to wonder where your own nosiness comes from surely? I mean I've never met anyone more inquisitive than you and that's saying something.'

Bella arrived to clear their plates and offered coffee. It was getting late but Viv ordered a double espresso knowing that she had a lot to do when she got home.

Mac said, 'Expecting a long night?'

'You know me too well.'

'I might be able to help.'

She tried not to look too interested. 'By doing what?'

'By renewing your access to the NTF data base.'

She fingered a stray crumb on the table.

He snorted, 'Oh, I see, you've already found a way round that.' He sighed, 'What am I to do to keep my system safe?'

'Employ me to build your walls. The thing is that by the time you guys have your super safe systems in place we on the dark side have already poked holes in them. You've got your finger in a very large dyke.' She sniggered, 'We'll always be ahead of the game. Oh, and if you think I'm one of a rare breed think again.'

'I know you're not but it seems stupid to be running round in circles trying to keep people like you out. Futile use of people power and . . .' He shook his head. 'What would your solution be?'

'Now why would I tell you that without a contract?'

'And I thought we were mates.'

'We are but you ask too much . . . If you ever need a hair cut let me know.'

Bella arrived with the coffees, 'You working an all-nighter?'

Mac laughed, 'See, it's not exactly rocket science. Even Bella's got your measure.'

Viv shook her head, 'Look you two, I'm on my way to a rave and 'til I get my recreationals . . .'

Mac scraped his chair back and made for the gents. 'Not hearing this, no way.'

Bella and Viv laughed, 'I knew that would get him. He's a by-the-book kind of bloke.'

Bella said, 'And you know how to wind him up big time.'

'Goes with the territory.' She sipped her espresso then stirred some sugar into it. 'This'll blow my head off.'

Bella grinned, 'I thought that was the point.'

Mac returned, glanced from one woman to the other and shook his head.

'It's a conspiracy.' He sipped his flat white and did the same as Viv, stirring in a spoonful of sugar. 'So what is your next move?'

'I'll find out a bit more about the petty thief, Jimmy Taylor. He might be working for someone else.'

Mac nodded. 'If you do need anything give me a shout.'

She smiled and leaned across to rub his hand. 'You are very patient and gracious with me. Thank you, it's much appreciated.'

He laughed, 'Patronising sod!'

She swigged the remains of her coffee. 'You done? I'd better get back to research.'

He wiped his mouth and gestured to Bella for the bill. 'Been an interesting week.'

She leaned forward onto the table, 'Anything more that would interest me?'

He matched her move. 'You're already interested.'

'Spill then.'

'Well, it'll hit the headlines tomorrow that someone on high is for the chop.'

She smirked, 'What will the headline say?'

'"Police Commissioner retires after health scare", or some other platitude.'

'Was the stick helpful? He surely knows that the additional info would be inadmissible.'

He glanced around, 'Sure he knows. But imagine the slur. You'll work out from the article. Read between those lines.'

'Be like that then. Let's get going.'

Mac wandered over to his car and Viv started back the way she'd come. 'I've eaten too much.'

He laughed, 'You'll work it off with all that brain power. By the way if you're worried about your fitness, you could come with me on Sunday. I'm doing a 5K for charity.'

She stopped, 'You are kidding?'

'No. You'd love it. A good run in the countryside. Think of all that fresh air.'

'It would kill me. Not the run, the fresh air. What charity?'

'You can choose. I'm raising for a local food bank.'

'I'll think about it and let you know.'

'So is that a "no" then?'

'Piss off. I said I'd think about it.' She grinned, waved and walked on.

Chapter Six

She brushed her teeth, changed into pjs, then settled into her cubbyhole and booted up her secondary screens. Jimmy Taylor and Kurt Hahn weren't the only people she wanted to know about. Although patience wasn't her greatest virtue she did have it if she was hooked by something. In the interest of deferred gratification she made a start on stuff she knew she couldn't access easily.

First up, the petty criminal turned window cleaner. From what she could see he really was petty. He'd never ventured beyond theft from supermarkets and a few break-ins where he definitely knew the people were away. Why would he stick his neck out for someone else? Money. Always follow the money. She found his Facebook profile and tracked a few leads but nothing interesting came up. He was a Hibernian supporter, and a good many of his posts were to do with footie. She checked his photographs. Sad. Not much in the way of family. Then she spotted an image of Jimmy in a box at Easter Road with a few Edinburgh worthies. She enlarged the shot. Jimmy was standing off to the side with his hands behind his back. Looking as if he was on duty of some kind. He wasn't big enough to be in the muscle department but he was definitely not just one of the group. She recognised another of the men as a serious patron of the club and of the Catholic Church. What the hell was Jimmy doing there? Usually he'd be on the terraces like most punters.

She wrote a few notes and copied the photograph to her laptop. She glanced up from the screen, pleased with her new room. The ceiling was so close to her head that she'd have to consider another name for it. It was smaller than a broom cupboard and had no natural light. Sulkery. It could be her sulkery. If Dickens could have a growlery she could have a sulkery. She shook her head. Sulkery or not she'd better keep her head down.

Kurt Hahn was much more interesting. No sign of a partner. Making a name for himself in the USA. Done a few tours in the UK but the press hadn't been very complimentary: 'We hate a plink plonker masquerading as a proper pianist.' She whispered, 'Serves him right for not researching his audiences.' Choosing a whole programme of uber modern pieces wasn't ever going to go down well, unless people were buying into the emperor's new clothes. She jotted down things that were slightly odd.

Eventually, just when she was about to call it a day she found a gem; a newspaper article that had gone viral about Kurt having a punch-up with a man in the foyer of a concert hall in Berlin. The journalist speculated at the end of the piece that the other man may have been Kurt's brother. Interesting. What causes two brothers to fight? Is a different question from, what causes two brothers to fight in such a public space, the prestigious environment of a concert hall? Was one brother trying to humiliate the other?

She rubbed her eyes and checked the time: 1.30am. Better hit the hay. Her mobile pinged a message coming in. It was Sal's number. She read the text. 'Have had a message from Brian, Mollie not well. Worried sick.' She replied, 'I'll find out in the morning and go up. Are you ok otherwise?' The phone rang.

Sal said, 'Oh, thank God you're still awake. It's not like Brian to send me a message. He must be really worried. The vet has taken blood samples but we'll not know the results until tomorrow.'

'Don't fret. If Moll's been to the vet that's the best Brian can do. I'll ring him in the morning and go up if necessary.'

Sal sobbed, 'I should be with her.'

'She's used to you being away. If Brian's busy I can look after her.' The words were out before she'd really thought it through. Moll would hate being in the city.

'Oh, would you? I'll be able to sleep if I know someone is with her round the clock.'

Viv hadn't said round the clock, but would do what she could. 'How are you otherwise?'

'It's so different . . . And I'm shattered from the flight. I'll settle in, I suppose.'

Not sounding at all like the Sal that she knew and loved. 'Look I'm just dabbling around in research. I can do that anywhere. Maybe I could stay at the cottage for a couple of nights?'

Sal's relief was audible, 'Really? But you hate the country side.'

'It'd be taking a hit for the team.'

Sal laughed.

Viv, relieved, said, 'She'll be fine. Brian and I will make sure of that. You try and concentrate on the job or they'll think they've hired a dud.'

Viv's brain was working nineteen to the dozen sorting the logistics of a couple of nights in Doune, the back of beyond.

Sal said, 'I am not a dud.'

'No one said you were. I said . . .'

'I know, I know. I'm just touchy. I will have to concentrate on work. They've already assigned me to a project.'

'Interesting.'

'Yes, but not for now. I'll speak to you tomorrow if I get the chance.'

'I won't get up there until lunch time, but I will catch Brian first thing.'

They rang off and Viv rubbed her hands roughly over her face. If she went to the cottage she'd only have her laptop for work. She reminded herself that until a couple of weeks ago she'd worked perfectly well with 'only' a laptop. Defo time for some shut-eye. In bed she tossed and turned, kicked off the duvet, retrieved the duvet, got up to pee, had a glass of water. Eventually, slept like the dead.

Chapter Seven

Friday

A dream just before she'd woken up remained with her as she chewed on a slice of toast. She'd texted Brian and was waiting for a reply, but images from the dream kept reappearing. She'd been with Dawn and Mollie on Lothian Road waiting for a bus or a taxi. She couldn't remember which. It was a warm summer day and all was good with her and Dawn. Somehow, as is the case with dreams, Fortnum and Mason's was at the bottom of the road and she decided to leave Dawn and go shopping. She was in such a good mood as she sauntered in through the front atrium of the shop and took the very narrow escalator to the first floor. She passed through a huge café where lots of people were having posh afternoon tea, their plate racks stacked with goodies. She exited through large glass doors onto a balcony where people were sunbathing. She became aware that she was naked, but wasn't too worried other than about being too pale.

After a few minutes meandering along the balcony, with other naked people lying sunbathing but not interested in her, she returned to the shop and took the escalator to the next floor. At the top a box of smart olive oils prevented her from getting off and an assistant had to come to her aid to remove the box. She then took the escalator back to the ground floor and out onto Lothian Road again, where the mood was decidedly different. With no sign of Dawn or the dog she felt her belly tighten.

This was exactly as it had been with Dawn. One minute all beautiful in the garden, the next black clouds racing over and all hell let loose. Now as she swallowed her toast she realised how much fear had been invested in that relationship and how different, how loving it was with Sal. Her mobile vibrated on the worktop; it was Brian's number.

'Hi Brian, how is she?'

'She's still with the vet. They kept her overnight because she was so dehydrated. They think it could be some kind of toxin. She's been licking her paws a lot so I asked if it could be salt that's been spread on our lane. We don't usually get it, but someone has been out in the last few days and spread a load of it over the bridge and up the lane towards the castle. The vet's not sure yet. Apparently some councils put anti-freeze in their road salt. That wouldn't be good.'

This was the most she'd ever heard Brian speak.

'Sal is worried.'

'Yeah, I know. She knows I've got a family funeral and will have to go to it.'

'Okay. I'll come up.'

'You could wait until I hear from the vet again. Actually there's another caller trying to get through.'

He cut the call and she waited.

Her mobile vibrated almost immediately. 'That was them, she's getting out. I've to pick her up as soon as. She's to be kept quiet and . . .'

He sounded stressed.

Viv interrupted, 'I've got a few things to do this morning, but I'll come up after that. I can work from the cottage.'

'Well, if it's no bother?'

She smiled, 'No, it's no bother. See you later. Oh, by the way, is the heating on at the . . .'

'Of course. Doctor Chapman keeps it on round the clock.'

'Right. See you later.'

The cottage was beautiful, comfortable and cosy so it wouldn't really be a hardship to be there, apart from the silence. Who could live without sirens? She checked her emails and answered a couple that were urgent. One from Jinty who said, 'Phew! Concert went well, or wellish, and he's left for London.'

Jinty must have been pretty worked up about him and his questioning her to be this relieved to see the back of him. Better factor in another conversation with her about exactly what he wanted to know. Jinty wasn't flighty. She was grounded, and if she was worried there must have been good reason. She sent a quick email back trying to fix a time for coffee. No immediate reply meant she'd missed her window. Jinty was a slacker in the social media department; only checked and compiled emails once a day.

Viv had clients to see, a husband and wife team to cut, before she could take off to Doune. She threw essentials into a bag: seven pairs of pants and her toothbrush, a couple of tees and spare trousers, socks, and finally her laptop and a specific note pad.

She was going to the north-west of Edinburgh. She could park in one of the wide leafy streets for a maximum of an hour. She'd have to be quick, but Joseph and Marie, not as biblical as they sounded, were always ready when she arrived. Both worked from home and were relaxed about taking twenty minutes out to have a haircut. Just as she expected Joseph opened the door and invited her in. His hair dripped onto a towel wrapped round his shoulders. He led her to the kitchen and she set up. The house was full of interesting bits of modern art, more at the crafty end than fine, but always interesting. A bowl with an iridescent bluish glaze sat on the kitchen table burgeoning with tangerines still with their leaves attached. Dragon's heads, or were they gargoyles, rose up from its base their tongues lolling. Joseph and Marie both worked in graphic design. Viv was never sure exactly what that meant, but they were switched on about any exhibitions that were worth seeing.

Joseph sat. 'Marie will be ready in a minute.'

Viv noticed a flyer for the Kurt Hahn concert on the worktop, 'Did you go to hear him?' She gestured with her head towards the flyer.

'Yes, we did. Interesting.'

Viv smiled, 'Interesting, as in not very?'

Joseph nodded, 'Not our kind of thing in the end. Recommended by a friend who is usually on the money with his recommendations, but not so with the pianist. He seemed tense all the way through. You've got to expect a performer to be tense for a few minutes until they get into their stride, but he was rigid all the time. At the end he scanned the audience and the exits as if he was expecting to be . . . oh I don't know. Anyway, how are you Viv? I'm guessing you didn't attend.'

'No, but I met him with another client and as you say he was tense.'

Joseph's hair was short and dark, his hairline beginning to recede, and with flecks of grey at the temples, but he was a striking looking man who could get away with any cut. Marie joined them and put the kettle on.

'Coffee?'

Viv glanced up, 'Not for me, thanks. Already buzzing.'

'Joe?'

'Sure, I'll have some.'

Marie, tall with golden hair and a clear pale complexion looked like a Celtic goddess. Everything about her was slender; her hips, legs, fingers looked as if they might break at any moment. Viv wondered what their children would be like. Not that there was any sign of them having children. But sometimes there was just too much beauty and nature kicked it into touch with the next generation.

Marie said, 'I heard you mention the concert. Did you go?'

'No, sadly I didn't.'

'Oh, not sadly at all. If we hadn't been with a friend we'd have left at half time.'

'We would not. We'd have given him the benefit of the doubt.'

Marie glared at her husband. 'Well you might not have but I would. It was the most ghastly performance we've been to in a long time. Even Ricky was disappointed.'

'Ricky is always disappointed.'

Marie handed him a mug of coffee.

He gripped it but it was too hot to hold and he laid it on the table. Marie lifted it and put a coaster underneath.

The tension in the kitchen rose a notch, but Joe didn't say anything. Once the drier was on all opportunity for chatter was gone. Viv finished off his hair with a touch of pomade.

Joseph said, 'Thanks, Viv. Looks great, as ever.' Then sloped off into his office with his mug of coffee.

Marie sat down lightly on the vacant chair. 'Right, time for a change. What do you think?'

Viv had been through this so many times with Marie that she smiled and said, 'Okay, how about graduation round the front?'

'How will that be when I put it up?'

'Should be fine, but you'll probably have the odd tendril fall loose.' She knew this would clinch the no-change deal.

'Oh, I hate having bits falling onto my face. Let's just stick with what we've got, only a bit shorter.'

'How much is a bit?'

Marie held her finger and thumb about a centimetre apart. 'That much.'

So less than Viv would take off normally. 'Okay, no problem.' She wrapped a gown round Marie's shoulders and continued to section off the back. Viv could divide her clients into compliant and non-compliant. Marie was the latter, so when Viv tried to gently push her head to one side to get tension on the hair before cutting it Marie resisted. After two or three attempts Viv said, 'Could you just put your head slightly to the right?' Still resistant. Didn't make for an accurate cut but what could Viv do? Doing the best job she could in the circumstances. She said, 'So did you know anything about Kurt Hahn before the concert?'

'Only that he was an amazing pianist who rarely comes to Scotland. In fact, I'm not sure it wasn't his first time playing here. Never again.' She said it with emphasis. 'Never again would I sit through that racket.'

Viv laughed, 'Interesting what some people think of as music.'

'I'm telling you it was as if he was being tortured. Who'd have known that a piano could produce such horrid sounds.' Marie shook her head in disgust. 'Anyway, what's new with you, Viv?'

'Oh, just ticking along. Managing to get most people fitted in before the Christmas break. Are you here or away?'

'Supposed to be going to my family. Big grumbles about that though. Joseph says we always go to mine, but it isn't true.'

Viv wasn't keen to be drawn into a domestic so changed the subject. 'Off to Milan in the spring again?'

Marie brightened, 'Yes. Can't wait.'

'What exactly is it you do there?'

'Oh, it's just a chance for techies to get together and share what's new.'

Viv liked the sound of that. 'D'you have to be invited?'

'God no, anyone can go. The more creative the better.'

Viv finger-dried Marie's golden tresses, since the hairdryer made them frizz, then was on her way with her fee already transferred directly into her account.

Next stop her mum's, which was only five minutes away. She parked where she always parked, trotted to the door and pressed the buzzer to her mum's flat. No answer. She tried again, still no answer. She walked round the side of the building to where Mand had parked and looked up at her mum's windows. Curtains still drawn. This was completely out of character. Her mum was an up, showered and dressed with breakfast before 8am kind of woman. She returned to the front door and someone was leaving, so she slipped into the building and ran up to the first floor and rapped on the door. She heard a noise inside and said, 'Mum, it's Viv.'

There was movement and a bit of a kerfuffle before her mum eventually unlocked the door and held it open.

'What the heck?'

Her mum's clothes drying horse was lying on the floor partially propped against the entrance to the bathroom.

'What's that doing there?'

Her mum folded the three sections into one and put it in the bathroom. 'I just thought it would keep the door jammed shut.'

'But why do you need it jammed shut?'

Her mum turned away and shrugged, then sighed, 'Oh I think someone's tried the door at night. I know you think I'm being paranoid but . . .'

'No, I don't think you're being paranoid at all. I'll ask to see the CCTV.'

'No, don't do that. I don't want to draw attention to myself. And I don't want whoever it is to know that you know.'

This was mad. 'But if you're unsafe of course we'd have to know. You moved into this ghastly place to be safe, to get away from the horrid neighbour who kept bugging you. There's no point moving from the frying pan . . .'

Her mum interrupted her, 'I know. I just think this needs careful handling.'

'And what exactly is "this"?'

The older woman sank onto her small two-seater couch and picked at her nails. 'I can handle this, Viv. There's no need for you to get involved.'

'Yeah sure, you might have got away with that a decade ago but not now. Tell me what's going on.'

A buzzer rang and her mum's forehead crumpled in concern.

'I'll get it.' Viv pressed the button to hear the caller. It was Mand. 'Hi, in you come.'

'It's Mand, you can relax. I'll stick the kettle on and you can tell us both.'

'I've nothing to tell. But there's shortbread in the tin.'

Viv shook her head as Mand walked in the door carrying James and two huge bags, 'essentials' for a toddler. It seemed he needed more for one day out than Viv would need for a month away.

Mand dumped the bags and handed James to her mum.

Viv said, 'Mum was just about to tell me what's been going on.'

'So, Jamesie, how was play group?' Their mum shoogled James on her knee, clearly determined to avoid eye contact. Whatever the conversation had been before it was now over. The phone rang and she flinched, almost losing the boy off her lap. Mand leapt to the rescue but her mum recovered and got James in hand. She didn't answer the phone. It rang and rang and rang. She continued to shoogle James and blether about nothing of consequence. Viv and Mand stared at each other in disbelief. As soon as it stopped ringing Viv checked the number of the last caller. Number withheld. Could have been a sales call but Viv wasn't convinced. Viv's own mobile vibrated, and she checked the number. It was Mac.

'Hi, how are you?'

'Fine. Just wanted to let you know that a man's body was found in the canal this morning.'

'I'm guessing they weren't in swimming or part of a rowing team?'

'No, inevitable dog walker spotted something beneath the ice. If she hadn't been scrabbling at the side of the bank trying to reach her dog's ball it might have been days before he was found. What would we do without dog walkers?'

'How did he die?'

'Not certain yet but he doesn't look bonnie and not just because he's a bit bloated. Looks as if he's had an argument with a car and the car won. But don't quote me on that. PM will take a couple of days. There's been a spate of unexplained deaths. Thought you'd like to know though it'll be on the news this morning. He looks like your guy Jimmy, although difficult to be sure. Odd don't you think, that you were just talking about him and he turns up dead?'

'Shit! Whereabout on the canal?'

'Wester Hailes. Not his patch. He's a Leither. Did you say you would do that run with me?'

'No, I did not, so don't push your luck. Thanks for the heads up.'

Mand had made tea and brought shortbread while Viv was on her phone. The house was stifling as usual and she loosened her scarf and jacket. How did her mum stand it?

Mand shot Viv a quizzical look, 'Anything that I might like to know?'

Viv glanced at the elderly woman sitting there in her beige summer lights and tried to comprehend the possibility of her having been some kind of operative. Looking at her now, she'd lost weight but looked fit, her forearms sinewy, fingers long and strong, not gnarled like many women of her age. But Viv didn't think that she could run fast even if she needed to. How would she know though? She only ever saw her mum indoors these days. In that moment she had the craziest idea. 'How about we all have a bit of quality time away?'

Mand looked shocked. 'Away away? You, me, mum and James away?'

Viv nodded, 'Sure. You, James, mum and I. Just for the weekend. What do you say mum?'

'I say you must be mad. I'm not going anywhere. You three go, though. I'll be fine.'

This was not part of Viv's plan, but she'd like to find a way of convincing her mum that it was just a jolly and not an escape.

Their mum continued to chat to James until eventually the sisters realised that there was no way that she was going to speak about whatever was going on.

Viv let go of a huge sigh, 'Right, well, if you're not interested in some family bonding I'm off. Sal's dog is ill and I said I'd look after her.'

'Really. Where's Sal?'

Mand knew little of Viv's life so she was intrigued by the question, which pre-supposed there had been a conversation between Mand and someone else, perhaps their mum, about Viv's love life. 'She's in the States.' Suitably vague.

Mand pressed, 'For work or play?'

'Work.'

'Does she still have her place near Dunblane?'

'Doune,' Viv corrected automatically, then could have kicked herself for being so specific. 'Right, I'll be off. You've got my mobile if you need me.'

Before leaving the building she made a visit to the warden's office. There was a note on the door reminding people of her office hours and ONLY in an emergency was she to be disturbed outside of those times. Viv reckoned this was emergency enough and rang the buzzer at the side of the door. No answer. She tried again. Nothing. Viv cursed. What did she get paid for?

The journey to Doune took fifty minutes. She waved at each speed camera as she sailed by over the limit. As she turned into the lane leading to Sal's cottage, she dropped her shoulders and cracked her head from side to side. She felt sluggish. Time to up her fitness regime. Babysitting for a dog would be the least demanding thing she'd done in ages; plenty of free time to jog around the estate. Poor Molly did at least stand up to greet her as she entered the cottage, but soon returned to the comfort of her basket by the Aga. Brian had left a note on the table with sachets of stuff to put in her water bowl to rehydrate her. No exercise for a couple of days, and small amounts of food often rather than a large amount at once. 'I can do that, Moll. You and I are going to be just fine.' The dog banged her tail on the floor at the side of her bed. At least she was trying to be enthusiastic.

Viv set up her laptop in the conservatory where Brian had laid the wood burning stove ready to be lit. She wandered back to the kitchen area and put the kettle on. She hadn't got the hang of the Aga, which took up a huge amount of space, but was delighted when it was on since it became the beating heart of the house. Sal was convinced that once you'd had an Aga there was no going back to an ordinary cooker, but that didn't stop her from having a sort of Baby Belling type oven and hotplate as well.

'So here we are Moll, just the two of us.'

The dog licked Viv's fingers but didn't venture far from her bed.

Viv reread her instructions and imagined Brian would be round as soon as he got back from the funeral. Sal kept a fully stocked larder and her freezer could feed the five thousand. Quite the opposite of Viv, who ate out most of the time and whose cupboard was always bare. It was weird being in Sal's home without Sal there. Viv opened and closed cupboards as if she might find her hiding in one of them. By the time she'd made tea her computer was booted up and she emailed Sal to say that she'd arrived and Moll seemed to be on the mend. It didn't take long for the dog to come through and lie across Viv's feet as she clicked away at the keys. Must be where Sal worked.

When Viv next lifted her head, the light was beginning to fade. She'd promised herself she'd run at least a couple of miles before dark. It took more will power than it should have to move the dog from her comfy position, but needs must and Moll went back to her cosy spot by the Aga when Viv went upstairs with her bag to change. She warmed up in the hallway with a few stretches then ran round the field directly outside the cottage. It was called the River Park for obvious reasons. Two sides were flanked by rivers: the Ardoch, more of a burn unless it was in spate when it turned into a torrent, the other the Teith, a major tributary of the Forth and a serious salmon river that locals didn't want known about for fear of it becoming as over-fished as the Spey. It took her a few minutes to get into her stride but once she found it she ran on and on. There was a good loop that took her almost to Dunblane where she could return along an old railway line, a dog walker's paradise and consequently she had to keep a close watch where she was treading. In less than forty minutes she was running back along the lane and over the humpbacked bridge before turning in through the estate gates and up the drive.

She heard Moll bark as she approached. Odd she hadn't barked when she'd arrived earlier. Maybe she'd heard some other country noise or was seeing off an imaginary foe. But not so; there was another car parked in the drive. Viv could only see a small section of its boot but she'd swear it was Mand's Lexus. It was. Mand, her mum and James, asleep in the back of the car, sat waiting. WTF?

Viv gaped in the window and Mand got out, 'Hi sis, I managed to persuade mum that we needed a break together.' She winked at Viv.

Viv stood with her hands on her hips trying to get her breath back. She wiped her face on her tee shirt, 'Excellent. Come on in. Oh, and best not let James near the dog.'

'He's asleep. But anyway he'll be fine with her.'

'He might well be fine with her but she's not well and I'd rather she wasn't stressed.'

Let the tension begin.

Chapter Eight

Viv pushed back the front door and stood aside to let Mand carry in a waking James with their mum following.

Their mum said, 'Got your way after all.' Nice greeting. 'I hope there's plenty of space for us. I like my own space.'

Viv shook her head and blew out a huge breath, regretting her suggestion without having thought through the logistics. How had Mand known where to come? Where would she find the bed linen? There were beds for all. Mand could have a few cushions on the floor for James if need be. As it turned out Mand had brought everything but the kitchen sink, including a blow-up mattress for James. Suddenly the house felt tiny. The clutter in the hallway had to be dispersed to bedrooms and James's kit spread between the bathroom downstairs and the one upstairs. Viv had to let Sal know that her house had been taken over by the Frasers. She ran the tap and drank a long cold glass of water, then clicked the kettle on.

Mand said, 'You do know that the point of an Aga is that it does everything, including boiling the kettle?' She glanced around the kitchen and when she spotted it she filled the proper kettle and set it to boil on the hotplate, switching off the other one at the wall. Viv sensed that now was not the time to start to fight over a kettle, but also knew that the weekend ahead wouldn't be a picnic.

Her mum, determined to remain independent, wouldn't let Viv carry any of her bags, especially not the large and heavy-looking tapestry one up to the spare room at the back of the house. It was a lovely room but was chilly since there hadn't been any heating on. Viv crawled behind the curtain and found the thermostat for the radiator. 'I'd have had all this sorted if I'd known you were coming.' Luckily the beds were made up, but Viv left her mum to settle in and went in search of towels for everyone. What had she done? Would she get any work done now? Better not fret about it yet; they'd only been there five minutes.

Once she'd set the towels in each room she went down to the kitchen where Mand had made a pot of tea and was crouched down on the floor with a mug in one hand and Moll's belly occupying the other. A tender sight that made Viv well up. Was it because the dog was so trusting? Had she lost sight so much of Mand that she only saw the bitter bits?

Mand said, 'She's a sweetie. I bet she's missing her mummy.'

This had occurred to Viv, but hearing someone else saying it made it more real. Maybe the dog's sickness was in her heart and not in her body. It was entirely possible.

'I know it's getting late but I bet you haven't eaten. I could make pasta for supper.' She opened the fridge, pulled out a block of parmesan and checked the sell-by date on it. It was fine. There was tagliatelle and a couple of tins of tomatoes. That would do. Sal had a vast selection of dried herbs, none of which Viv would have used had she not had company. She refilled the kettle and set it on the hotplate.

Mand smiled.

'I'm a fast learner.'

'I've no doubt you are, but it's a first for you doing anything that I'd recommend.'

'That's bollocks. I'm happy to take advice.'

'Yes, I'm sure that's true, but not from me you're not. But let's not fight about it. I'm just glad to see you conserving energy.'

Viv hauled down a large pot from a hook above the Aga and searched for a grater.

Mand saw it first and held onto it. 'Here, let me.' She took the parmesan over to the table and grated it into a bowl. Viv chopped up a clove of garlic that she found in the fridge door and opened the tins of tomatoes. Their mum joined them in the kitchen.

'Nice to see you two at work together.'

Viv and Mand looked at each other, then at their mum.

Viv said, 'And your point is?'

'Well, every time you come to me you're at loggerheads. So all I'm saying is that it's nice to see you doing something together peacefully. When you were young you were always protective of each other.' She stared out of the window into a dense velvety blackness. 'This is a lovely home. Private, secluded, safe.'

Viv was intrigued by her mum's observations. Were those things her priorities now? It was true that Sal's cottage was homely, but so was Viv's flat. Not that her mum had visited it. She tried to recall the last time the three of them had stayed under the same roof and couldn't think of a single time since their dad had died. Wow. This *would* be an interesting weekend.

Viv banked up the woodburning stove and they ate a passable dinner. Moll seemed brighter with company and had eaten a little bit of her food. She was also drinking water with the sachets from the vet. So far so good. After they had eaten they went into the conservatory and Viv drew the curtains to make it cosier. She shut down her laptop so that they couldn't accuse her of 'always working', their most frequent war cry.

'So, mum, how about you give us a clue as to what's going on?'

Her mum stared at her, 'However hard you try to wheedle it out of me, this is not my story to tell.'

'Maybe not, but is it your secret?'

Her mum inclined her head as if conceding the point to Viv. 'What I can say is that it all began a long time ago and it's about time it was put to bed. When I've figured it out I'll let you know. In the meantime tell Sal thanks for letting us stay in her beautiful home.'

While their mum was speaking, Mand stared at her feet.

Viv didn't give up easily. 'Don't you think there's some merit in getting help. For starters, Mand and I are fitter than you.'

Her mum swept her hand in the air, 'You don't know anything, Vivian.'

The 'Vivian' was not a good sign, only used on high days and holidays or if she was out of favour.

'No matter what you think we are fitter than you.'

'You think?' Her mum set her mug on a side table, lay down on the floor and proceeded to do ten powerful push-ups without any sign of exertion.

Mand joined her mum on the floor and Viv shook her head but did the same, and the three women proceeded to do push-ups until each of them had had enough. Viv did manage a few more than she thought she would, but there was nothing like a bit of competition from a parent to spur her on. In the end they lay side by side breathing hard until their mum stood up and started doing star jumps.

'Okay, okay, I think we get the picture. You've been practising, which is cheating.'

'It's not about practice, Vivian, it's a way of life.'

'I don't remember you doing anything like that when we were growing up.'

'No, you wouldn't. You went to bed or I went to work.' The slightest of smiles crept across her face as if a fond memory was awakened.

'You want to fill us in on that job?'

Their mum's face changed rapidly into a scowl. 'You know exactly what I did.'

It was Mand's turn to question. 'No, we don't.' She stared at Viv for confirmation.

Viv said, 'No, we don't. So what exactly was it you did?' If her mum had been an operative she'd be able to lie flawlessly to most people, but perhaps her family would prove to be an exception.

'I worked as a secretary in the Civil Service. I was lucky. Women before me had to give up work when they had children and some before that had to give up work altogether when they got married. I got in just . . .'

'So what exactly did you do as a secretary?'

There was the slightest of falters, 'I did the most dull, menial typing and . . .' Again her face changed as if another fond memory had been awakened. 'I had a good boss.'

'Ah, so who was that?' She had to get some detail. Her mum certainly wasn't working out the rota for the bin men.

'Oh, I can't remember his name now.'

Her first blatant lie.

'Okay. But you must remember where you worked.'

'Yes, yes. I worked in Government House at the east end of Princes Street.'

This sounded too vague, but Viv could easily find out.

'Which department?'

'You're pushing your luck, lady. I think I'll have an early night.'

Viv had been thinking the same thing since the push-ups. There was always tomorrow.

As their mum left the room, Mand gave Viv the thumbs up. 'Well done. If she's that uncomfortable talking about it she must have something to hide. Get your laptop booted, we have research to do.'

Viv hadn't seen Mand this excited for ages. She opened the laptop and Googled 'Government House Edinburgh'. The only thing close was a Governor's House on Calton Hill, but nothing close to Government House. The Governor's House had been part of the Old Calton Jail at the back of St Andrew's House, which definitely was a Scottish Government building. If they kept staff records that went back twenty-five or thirty years there was no way they'd be digitised. Viv could foresee a visit to their archives. Research was such a wonderful cover, and she still had her ID cards for the press.

She glanced at Mand, who was chewing the inside of her cheek. 'You know what? I bet if you worked there you'd call it something different to what the public called it . . . If I find anything, what department should I try?'

'I don't know. With all this cloak and dagger stuff why not just try intelligence.' She snorted. 'By the way before you came along I spent a lot of time with grannie, much more than you ever did.'

Viv paused her search, surprised to hear this. She'd imagined their childhoods with much the same rhythm, but obviously not. She turned back to the screen, but tapped her chin instead of the keys. If their mum had been attached to intelligence they would have used an innocuous name, but each one she tried came up blank. She'd definitely have to visit.

Mand said, 'It's pretty hard to believe that she was involved in anything . . . you know like espionage.'

Viv shrugged, 'I can't imagine her having enough time. I mean we never felt deprived of her company. She was never away, well not for long.'

Mand interrupted, 'She did go away for a couple of trips that lasted . . . oh I don't know maybe a week. We were farmed out to grannie or friends. I think one time you were at Guide camp.'

'Guide camp? Shit! I'd well and truly buried that memory. I hated it. I cried to come home on the first night but they wouldn't let me. Oh, and they thought that by telling us ghost stories that would make it better. Total nuts. Wonder what happened to them. Sisters, weren't they?'

Mand grinned, 'Yeah, but not the kind of sisters we are.' She laughed. 'Great euphemism.'

'Oh my God, of course. They looked nothing like each other. Well, well, I missed that one.'

Mand said, 'I'm tired. I think I'll go snuggle up with James.'

'Sure, I've got a couple of . . .'

Mand brushed away the details of her sister's existence. 'Sure, Viv. Sleep well.'

Once Mand had gone upstairs Viv emailed Sal to let her know that her house had now been inundated by the Fraser clan.

Chapter Nine

Saturday

When Viv appeared in the morning Mand and James were on the couch watching something on TV and their mum was sitting at the kitchen table with her hands wrapped round a mug of coffee.

She nodded to a pot on the Aga. 'Plenty left.' She pushed her chair back as if she was getting up to do it for Viv.

'It's fine. Sit where you are, I can get it myself. Would you like a top-up?'

Her mum put a hand over the top of her mug. 'No thanks, I'm buzzing already.'

Viv had no idea what her mum had for breakfast these days, but was surprised by the strength of the coffee. Her mobile phone vibrated. She checked the caller ID. It was Mac.

'Hi, Mac, what can I do for you?'

'Just checking that you're up for the race on Sunday?'

Viv had no recollection of agreeing to the race, but knew that was how Mac worked.

He said, 'It's for a good cause.'

'How far is it?'

'You can do 5K, 10K, or 13K. C'mon, it'll be fun.'

'Since when was running uphill fun?'

'Ah, so you do remember. I'll pick you up at nine. The start's at nine-thirty.'

'Where is it? You do know that I'm at Sal's.'

'Thought you might be. All the more reason to do the race; it's across the Braes of Doune. Five-minute drive from Sal's.'

'What the hell? Nothing to lose. See you there at nine, no need to pick us up. Oh and by the way my mum and sister are here.'

'Great. The more the merrier; they can come along to support us. There'll be a catering tent for them to hang out in.'

'Not sure that my mum's in a hanging out sort of mood; she did twenty press-ups last night.'

'Wow! Then she can join us on the run.'

Viv laughed, but thought it was always a possibility. 'I'll ask her.'

'You serious?'

'Yes. Why not? She and Mand are in better shape than I am at the moment.'

'Excellent! Family outing. See you then.'

She walked out to the hallway and lowered her voice, 'Wait, Mac, I've got a favour to ask.'

'Sure. Shoot.'

'How would I get access to staff records of St Andrew's House?'

He hesitated, 'Current or past?'

'Past.'

'How far back?'

'Not sure. Say between twenty and thirty years ago.'

'You think your mum was a spy then?' He laughed. 'I think they're held in a storage facility. I can find out before you go off on a wild goose chase. Or worse, break through a firewall unnecessarily.'

'You know me too well. If you get anything before tomorrow give me a call, otherwise see you there at nine.'

She went back into the kitchen where her mum was doing a crossword.

'Keeping the old grey matter active, mum?'

'Ssh. Damn! I almost had it. No wonder I enjoy living alone.'

Viv stuck a couple of slices of bread into the toaster but Mand, who'd come to fill up her coffee mug, retrieved them from the toaster, put them in a wire rack, then put it on the hotplate. 'Saving energy, Viv. I'm guessing the toaster is there for emergencies, like when the Aga runs out of oil.'

'Happy to learn the art of the Aga. I've never been able to get my head round it.'

'Their mum said, 'Wonderful big things. The heart of the home.'

Mand and Viv looked at each other, confused. Viv said, 'Have you ever had an Aga?'

There mum said, 'Not personally, but I've had to cook on one.'

'And when was this?'

'Curiosity killed the cat, Vivian.'

Mand shrugged. 'I don't remember anyone we know having one.'

'No, you wouldn't.' Their mum never once lifted her head from the crossword.

This weekend might turn out to be one of the most informative times that they'd had as a family.

'Did Dad know how to work one?'

She sat with her pencil poised. 'I don't think so. If only he was here you could ask him.'

This was the first time that Viv's mum had sounded regretful about their dad's death.

'You must miss him, mum.'

'I do. But regret is a big investment. It's a good lesson, girls. Don't live a life that will earn you regrets. There's nothing to be done about them. Your dad and I had no regrets.'

This sounded more like a threat than a confession.

'Now that dad isn't around can you tell us what his job really was?'

She shook her head. 'He did his duty and was very brave. That's all you need to know.'

Like hell Viv thought, but she'd better tread carefully or she'd get nothing.

'But what was his duty? We . . .' she pointed at herself and then at Mand, 'thought he was a policeman. That's what we'd always been told.'

'He was a policeman. A special policeman. Remind me to show you some photographs I've got.'

'Where are they?'

Their mum had gone back to her crossword, but with an air of distraction said, 'Oh upstairs. I didn't like to leave them at home.'

Both Viv and Mand stood with eyes wide open. 'So is now a good time?'

'Have your toast and I'll show you.'

Mand had turned the toast over before it incinerated. Viv tried not to show her excitement but it was tricky with Mand giving the thumbs up behind their mum's back.

Viv was eager, but didn't want to rush things, so she said, 'Look, I'll go into the village and get fresh supplies, then we'll have food for the rest of the weekend and won't have to pilfer from Sal's larder.'

'Sounds good,' her mum said. 'Could you get me a newspaper?'

'Sure. *The Times*?'

'Yes, thanks.'

'Still reading about the old propaganda machine?' Her mum ignored her. 'What about you Mand, do you and James need anything specific?'

'I think I brought enough to see him through, but if they have . . . och it's fine if you're buying fresh veg I can make stuff with that.'

She glanced at Moll who was on the sofa in the conservatory with her chin resting on the arm, staring out of the window. 'You okay, Moll?' The dog was off the sofa in a beat and by Viv's side. Viv rubbed her ears and went in search of her lead. Unlike Sal she never took the dog for a walk without the lead on. Too nervous that Moll'd take off and she'd not get her back. The dog, clearly back to normal, spun round and round with excitement, so that Viv couldn't get the lead on her. 'Sit still.' Made no difference. Eventually Viv stroked her back, plonked her rear end on the floor and looped the lead over her head. 'Right, let's go.'

Moll trotted by her side as if being on a tether was normal to her. It was a crisp morning with blue sky and a thin layer of frost everywhere. The short walk to the village was charming. The lane flanked by specimen trees, a humpbacked bridge with the sound of the burn gurgling below it, the smell of organic matter mulching by the edges of gravel, everything contrary to her life in the city. She nodded to people she'd never met and replied when they bid her 'Good morning'. A man in a thick lumberjack shirt was petting Moll when she came out of the post office, a shop that sold everything. It was a good morning.

The main street in Doune supplied what she needed so she returned laden with food and essentials, the dog trotting by her side. She took a deep breath and got an inclination of what it was that Sal loved about living there. Sal was addicted to it. The rhythm was gentle, people in less of a hurry, and most of life's essentials could be found within a hundred paces of the house. What was not to like?

When she pushed open the door of the cottage, warmth and the smell of coffee made her imagine that maybe she could get used to country living. She'd always been averse to too much green. And maybe that was it – at this time of year the place was a lot less green. She dumped the bags on the kitchen table and began to unpack them. No sign of her mum, Mand or James. She heard water running upstairs so someone was in the shower. Note to self, don't run the cold tap or they'll get scalded. The fridge began to bulge with food, a much healthier sight than hers ever did at home. Eventually her mum appeared with the tapestry bag that she hadn't allowed Viv to carry upstairs for her.

Viv was itching to see what was inside, but they couldn't begin without Mand.

'Amanda hasn't come back yet?'

'Don't think so. There's been no sign of her.'

'She said she'd take James out, give him some fresh air and exercise to tire him out.'

'Poor wee soul, he's barely up.'

'Oh, he's been awake since five-thirty. He'll need a rest.'

Viv flipped the switch on the kettle then remembered to use the Aga. Her mum noticed and said, 'It'll become second nature.'

Viv wanted to ask how she knew if she'd only used one a couple of times, but zipped her lips. She handed the newspaper to her mum who immediately turned to the Obituaries. 'Someone you know died?'

She closed the paper and withdrew to the conservatory. 'That nose of yours will get you into trouble, Vivian.'

'How long have they been out?'

'They left more or less at the same time as you.'

'So what, about forty-five minutes, an hour?'

Her mum nodded, 'I suppose. Why?'

'No reason. Just it's freezing out there. I can't imagine what would take all this time.'

'If they're not back in half an hour you can go and find them. They won't have gone far.'

'The riverbank is slippery. They could have had an accident.'

'Much as you think Mand isn't as switched on as you I think you'll find since James came along her priorities have changed.'

Half an hour passed and Viv who was now doubly tetchy put her boots on and a lead on Moll.

'Be back soon. I'm going to walk the riverbank downstream. I'll come back here before I try anywhere else.'

Her mum gave her a curt nod. 'Okay. Is there a bell or a whistle?'

Viv started looking in the hall cupboard and the drawers of a cabinet. Her mum came through. 'I'll do that, you go down the river.'

Her mum not as relaxed as she'd been pretending to be. Moll, delighted to be on her second walk of the day, wagged her back end as if it would fall off. The riverbank was littered with mulching leaves, broken twigs and branches. The river, not as high as she'd seen it before, was still flowing at a fair pace. She watched a plastic juice bottle racing by, swept in spirals as it went. There was no sign or sound of Mand or James. After twenty minutes she returned via the Chapel Wood. There was plenty of light through the trees, nothing overgrown and the ground a carpet of dead leaves. If they were there she'd definitely be able to spot them. The crack of her footsteps onto twigs and bracken was the only thing interrupting the quiet. Moll went off sniffing madly towards a hollow. A roe deer broke cover and Viv almost had heart failure. It was out of sight so fast that she could hardly believe it had been there. 'Well done, Moll.' She tried to stroke the dog's head but Moll's nose was busy on the ground. Mand and James couldn't have been this way otherwise the deer wouldn't have settled. She arrived back at the house. She could see her mum inside the conservatory, standing with her arms crossed, her eyes scanning the fields.

Viv took off in the opposite direction, towards the village. As she approached the humpbacked bridge Moll began to strain at the lead. She was trying to get over the wall which led to the water. Viv hauled her back but leaned over the parapet and shouted, 'Amanda!'

She heard a reply, and scrambled over the wall and down the embankment. Mand and James were huddled at the edge of the archway beneath the bridge.

'What the hell?'

Mand tried to stand up but couldn't manage with James in her arms. Viv took hold of James and Mand was able to get to her feet.

'What are you doing down here?'

'Let's save it 'til we get back.'

Viv put James on her shoulders and helped Mand hobble up the bank. It was so slippery that they all fell down. Viv said, 'I'll take James up and come back for you.'

'No, no, don't leave him on his own.'

'Okay. Give me your hand. I'll edge up on my backside and pull you up.'

After a few minutes they made it to the top. All they had to do was scale the wall to get back onto the road. But the drop on this side was higher than from the road, so Mand had to stand on Viv's back to make it, then Viv handed James up to her as she sat on the wall. Moll managed the leap and Viv followed. Just a few metres away a tree had come down and was lying near enough to the wall to be used as a step. On the road they looked at each other. Mand's cream trousers and jacket were filthy. James wasn't too bad but had lost his hat. Viv was covered in mossy mud on all sides. They traipsed back to the cottage in loaded silence.

'We're back!' Viv shouted as she pushed open the front door. No answer. She deposited James on the rug in the hall and called out again, 'Mum, we're back.' No answer. 'Shit! Surely she hasn't gone out looking for you.'

Mand stripped off her outdoor kit then did the same with James.

'What happened? How come you were . . .'

Mand held up her hand, 'Mum'll want to hear as well so let's wait until she appears.'

They both stared at each other at exactly the same moment, then Mand shouted, 'Mum! Oh shit!'

Viv said, 'She can't have gone out. I've already been down the river looking for you.'

Mand said, 'I walked towards the village so that James could see the castle and so we wouldn't get dirty. Total joke. Look at us.'

'I don't need to. I need to find mum.'

Viv went to the back door and found it slightly ajar. There's no way her mum would leave the door open in this weather. She shouted into the garden, 'Mum!' No answer. She went back inside and grabbed her coat and boots. 'She can't have gone far. She's not dressed for being out in this weather. For God's sake, what is wrong with you people?'

Mand said, 'What the f . . .?' She glanced at James. 'She wouldn't go out without telling us unless it was an emergency.'

Reluctantly, 'I suppose, but she's behaving as if she's forty again and as much as people say seventy's the new fifty I'm not so sure . . .' She scratched her head. 'Why? What happened that you were under the bridge?'

'There was someone following us.'

Viv let go of a huge sigh, 'How do you know?'

'Well, we went along the lane to the castle and I happened to look back, and there was a man behind us. He looked away as if he was lighting a cigarette, but it just didn't look right. I told myself the same as you would, that I was being stupid, over-reacting. But when we'd had enough of the castle I saw him hovering in the car park, and when we were leaving he was behind us again.' She lifted James off the rug and pushed his hair back off his face. 'He was definitely following us and he didn't make a very good job of being discreet.' She ran a hand through James' hair again. He flinched and moaned. 'Sorry, sorry, sorry. Mummy didn't mean to be so rough.'

'Okay. You stay here and lock all the doors. I'll do another recce with Moll since she was the one to smell you guys on the other side of the wall. If mum comes back lock yourselves in. We've no idea who this crank is.'

Viv took off along the riverbank again and soon came across her mum walking towards her. No jacket and no outdoor shoes, one side of her trousers and her arm covered in mud. She was breathing hard but her colour was good and her eyes sparkling.

Viv opened her mouth to sound off, but her mum put a hand up to stop her.

'I'll explain back at the house.'

'You're damn right. You two are a complete liability. For God's sake we've only been together for a night. You shouldn't have left the house.'

Her mum marched ahead and nodded her agreement. 'But sometimes plans don't work out the way you thought they would, right?'

Viv banged on the door and Mand unlocked it and let them in. Their mum gave her an apologetic look, but Mand shook her head. 'What the hell were you thinking going out dressed like that?'

'I didn't mean to, but there was a man at the window so I went into the garden to ask what he wanted and he took off. I followed. He must be mad. He waded across the river. Did you see how high it was?'

'I don't care how high the river was, I care that you were stupid enough to go chasing a strange man. Look at you, you're not in any fit state to go out. It's freezing out there.'

Their mum shuddered. 'I might take a hot bath.'

'I'll get you a blanket until you stop shivering and you will tell us what the hell is going on. And how did they find us up here in the middle of nowhere?'

'They must have been watching my flat and followed us here. It's not rocket science.'

Viv's blood began to simmer. She bit down on her lip, 'Okay, stop right there. Who are "they"'?'

'I honestly don't know. But can probably find out.'

'Well, that's progress.' She nodded to Mand, 'You tell her what happened to you.'

Mand said, 'I was followed.' She glanced at Viv. 'I'm not making this up.'

Viv replied, 'No one thinks you are. Just tell us exactly what happened.'

'I took James to see the castle and on the way I saw a guy. He looked odd, as if he had stopped abruptly and turned away. Then I saw him do the same sort of thing in the car park at the castle. I felt nervous because James wouldn't stand still and kept wriggling away from me and trotting off. I can keep up with him but sometimes he bolts into spaces that I can't reach. I decided to give him a high shoulder and walk back. The guy was definitely behind us. So I shimmied over the wall and hid. That's when you found me.' She nodded at Viv.

'Describe him to mum. Maybe it was the same guy that she was chasing. Let's hope so, otherwise it means we're dealing with two.'

'Tall, heavy build, reddish blonde hair, smoker, leather jacket, black jeans or trousers.'

'No specific identifying features?'

Mand said, 'No. I didn't get that close.'

Their mum interrupted. 'I did. He has old acne scars and it sounds like the same guy. God knows how he didn't get swept away in the burn. But he didn't and he ran back up the opposite bank towards the village.'

'Did you recognise him, mum?'

Her mum hesitated. 'No. I don't think I did.'

'What do you mean you don't think you did? Either you did or you didn't.'

'No, then no I didn't.'

Viv, a super-recogniser, wasn't convinced but didn't push it. 'How did he get here without passing me on the lane? There's no way unless he went behind the castle farm, which is a quagmire.' She was thinking aloud. 'So what does he want, mum?'

Their mum gave a huge sigh. 'Oh, it could be a couple of reasons, but the top of the list, if I'm right, he thinks I've got something that belongs to him.'

Viv couldn't believe what she was hearing. Not one reason but two for her mum, in her dotage, to be pursued . . . She continued, 'And do you have something that belongs to him?'

'No. But he'll never believe me. Let's have a hot drink.'

Viv put the electric kettle on and when the others opened their mouths she put her hand up. 'I'm doing things my way and that includes the boiling of water. No buts.'

'Such a waste . . .'

Viv feigned uninterest. 'Once we've got drinks and whatever else you need to keep your butt in a chair for the next however long it takes, you can go through the stuff you brought, and fill us in on the details that we need to know. So get comfy, we're in for the long haul.'

Her mum stood up and still wrapped in a blanket went upstairs. After twenty minutes she returned in dry clothes and clinging onto the tapestry bag. She laid it on the floor in front of the sofa. James was immediately interested, but she drew it away from him and hoisted it onto her lap. She pulled out a box, slightly smaller than the one Viv and Mand had found beneath her bed, and a few large brown paper envelopes with old stamps on them but in good shape. She'd obviously treasured them. They hadn't been torn open; they'd been opened neatly using a knife or a letter opener. Mand held James on her lap and Viv sensed his frustration at not being allowed to play around on the floor. He was a strong little boy who wasn't easily deterred. Once he'd wriggled out of Mand's grasp he was happy and placed himself on the floor next to Moll and stroked her back.

The older woman gradually drew out papers from the box and photographs from the envelopes. Viv spotted a large photograph of her mum wearing a suit that could have been a parachute suit or a boiler suit of some kind. Whatever it was it was a coverall that emphasised her youth and her tiny waist. A woman also in military issue clothes stood at her side; they were both smoking cigarettes. She'd never imagined her mum like this, or in this kind of kit. All the pictures that were on display at home she was in a frock or twinset with a skirt. There were a couple of family pictures at the beach where everyone was wearing a swimsuit. Both her parents were in good shape and used to have swimming competitions and races along the wet sand when the tide was out. The more Viv thought of these things the more she realised that perhaps not all parents were as fiercely competitive with each other. The black and white image of her mum with the stranger was part of a life that she and Mand hadn't had access to.

The clothes of the woman in the photograph Viv had seen before since it hadn't changed much and was definitely military prison issue. Judging by her mum's modestly bee-hived hair the photograph had been taken in the late sixties, maybe early seventies. Their body language was not unfriendly, so who was the stranger and what was her mum doing with her? There were other papers, which her mum returned to the box without letting them see.

'What's up with those?' Viv gestured towards the box. 'Can't we get a look at those?'

Her mum stared at her. 'I'm not ready to let you see them.'

'So why did you bring them?'

'Because I don't want anyone to get their hands on them and for now that includes you.'

'I don't get why you need to be so secretive about things that happened a long time ago.'

'Don't you?' Again she stared at Viv.

Viv looked away.

'So you do know, but have one rule for you and another for me.'

Mand, who'd been looking through the photographs, stopped and glanced from one to the other. 'What's between you two? Sometimes I think you're more like enemies than family.'

Her mum answered, 'We're perhaps too alike.'

Viv snorted, 'I don't think so.'

Mand shook her head. 'That I think proves mum's point. You're just as stubborn or should I say determined as she is. You might as well get over it, Viv.'

What could be worse than your sister telling you how like your mum you are, when all your adult life you've done everything to oppose her and be like your dad? Viv slipped off the sofa onto the floor and joined James in stroking Moll, who rolled onto her back and enjoyed the attention. The dog was so at ease with James and he with her she wondered if Mand had given him a talk about how to behave with her. If not he was a natural, so sensitive and gentle she hadn't imagined him capable of it. She idly lifted up an envelope and pulled some photographs from inside. Tears immediately welled up at the black and white images of her dad, clearly taken just before the explosion. She couldn't bear to see them and put them back.

Her mum said, 'There'll be a right time for this and now is not it.' She scooped up most of the pictures and slipped them back where they'd been. She knew exactly which envelope each went into, and which belonged in the box and which didn't. There was definitely an order to all of this, and her mum had been its custodian for long enough to know it by heart. Viv didn't know the full story of her dad's death; she and Mand had been 'protected' from the details and told he'd died in the line of duty. She'd found out dribs and drabs about what her dad had done, but not the full extent of his work. Ruddy, from the NTF, had let slip that he'd worked with him, so Viv understood that he'd probably operated in intelligence at some point, but knew none of the details. Shit, did she actually come from a family of spies, as Mac had jokingly implied? Her belly clenched whenever she thought about seeking her dad's files. At one level she wanted the truth but at another she was still too raw to hear it. Seeing those photographs was proof of just how raw. She consoled herself; as her mum said, there would come a day.

Her mum's story, on the other hand, was more immediate. She was the person with a stalker. For someone to make the effort to follow her from Edinburgh to Doune they must imagine that whatever they wanted they thought she had with her.

Mand got James togged up and took him and Moll into the garden. 'Won't be long. I'll get us some proper fresh country air. It's stuffy in here.'

Viv watched from inside the conservatory as they wandered round exhausted flowerbeds. The dog set her snout to the ground and sniffed a million scents unavailable to humans. Mand crouched down and hugged James. She pointed to a Robin sitting on the branch of an Acer. James stood staring, his gloved thumb in his mouth, entranced by the sight of the tiny bird so close to him. Viv grabbed her phone and took a photograph then checked that she'd captured the moment before going in search of her laptop. She'd had two cups of coffee before she heard James squeal. She bolted back to the window but relaxed to see that all was well. It's a fine line between a fun squeal and one full of fear. Mand held James under his arms and was swinging him back and forth. He was almost hysterical with excitement. She was amazed at how finely attuned humans were without even knowing it. Mand clambered back in the door and began to peel off their layers of clothes and boots. Everything was a game for James's benefit and he chortled in response. It was such a joyful sight that Viv swallowed her emotion. People were constantly changing. No one stayed the same not even in death.

The light faded early and they spent the evening by the woodburner. Mand had James's entertainment down to a fine art. She allowed him short bursts on an iPad topped up by games and a singing competition, which he deemed Grannie to be the best since he asked her to sing the same song over and over again. Eventually exhaustion got the better of him and he lay beside Moll and dropped off to sleep. Another photo op.

Chapter Ten

Sunday

It was eight-thirty in the morning. Moll had picked up and was almost back to her old self. Viv was alerted to someone or something outside when the dog started running back and forth to the front door. It must be Mac approaching. He was early, but like Viv that was his preference. Viv pulled back the curtain in the bedroom and saw Brian's 4x4 in the drive. She nipped downstairs and after unravelling herself from the dog opened the door.

'Hi, Brian, come in.'

'No, you're all right. I just wanted to check that you were still here. And I see Moll's lookin' much better.' He scratched the dog's ears, as she nuzzled into his legs.

Viv felt a wave of something like guilt about her and her family muscling in on Sal's territory. She hadn't heard back from her so she didn't know if Sal was up to speed about what was going on back home. 'I've emailed Sal. She knows that we're all here.' She didn't know, but the lie fell lightly from her lips.

'Aye, she'll no mind. If you need me to do anything with Moll just geez a shout.' After kneeling to pet Moll he turned and went back to his pickup, which he had to reverse all the way down the drive since Viv and Mand's cars took up the whole width. Moll stood panting as he drove out of sight. Viv ruffled her ears. 'It's okay babe, you've got us. All females together.'

Clearly the dog understood the sentiment of her gesture because she trotted inside with Viv and settled into her basket. Viv hadn't noticed her mum standing at the Aga stirring a pot.

'Morning! What are you up to?'

'I thought I'd make porridge for the troops. If we're going to run up hills we'll need sustenance.'

Viv shook her head, 'You are kidding about us all going up the hill?'

Her mum frowned, 'Why would I kid about that?'

'Because you're in your . . .' The look her mum shot her was enough to stop her finishing her sentence.

'You weren't about to be ageist, were you?'

'No. No. I'll just go and get changed into my gear.'

'Wait! Actually I have something else to do this morning so I won't join you on the hill, but I'll be at the finishing line when you reach it.'

Viv was wary. 'Okay, so do we get to know what you're planning instead?'

'I'm going to church.'

Viv shook her head. She could see that her mum was hoping for a reaction. 'So what's made you find God all of a sudden?'

'Oh, I haven't, but it's a good place to catch up with old friends.'

Viv shook her head. 'Mum, what the hell are you up to?'

'I told you, nothing that I can't handle myself.'

'But you didn't handle Mand and James being followed, so it's obvious that you can't do it alone. Whatever it is you need help.'

'Okay. I didn't think they would take action so quickly.'

'Right! Enough with the "I'm a heroine" shit. We are all involved now. Who was the man in the photographs and is there any chance that he could still be alive?'

Her mum hurled round. 'No, there's no way he's alive and that's likely to be the problem, well part of it.'

'Great, so we're getting somewhere. And the other parts of the problem?'

She noticed the moment when her mother decided not to say anything more. 'Go and get Amanda. She'll need to eat if she's going to run.'

Viv ran her hands over her face and up into her hair, which she could have ripped out with frustration.

She took the stairs two at a time and knocked on Mand's door. It was difficult not to smile on hearing James giggling on the other side.

Mand said, 'Come on in. We're having fun getting dressed. James doesn't want to wear this.' She held up a sweater with one or other superhero on it. 'I only brought a couple of jerseys so he'll have to wear it sometime. Meantime he wants this one on.' Mand lifted him up and turned him round to show his lilac sweater with unicorns on it.

'Look at you, Jamesie. What a great jersey! I wish I had one.'

Mand raised her eyebrows. 'Thanks!' Sarcasm was her strong suit.

'You know that mum was planning on doing the run? Well, seems she's got something else on.'

'Really? We've already had Moll out for a walk. James is an early riser, as is mum, and she said she was going to give it a go.'

'Well, no need to worry since she's changed her mind.'

'For goodness sake, Viv, she's an adult. Whatever she wants to do we can't stop her. If you keep making a fuss it will only make her more determined. So chill and let's go and get some porridge. Remember she used to say it would stick to our ribs and make us strong.'

Viv recalled another event that involved porridge but she said, 'I'll get my kit on.'

We think we know our families and they think they know us, but we don't and they don't. People have selected highlights from the years that they were under the same roof; nothing more. Most of our adult lives are spent away from our families, and what we hang onto is the early stuff, not the continually-becoming-someone-different stuff. Viv had made her mind up about Mand long ago, and was now getting the sense that she was off the mark. She'd never have believed that Mand, with her immaculate hair, manicured nails and glamour regime, would enjoy the outdoors.. As for their mum, WTF? She'd boxed her mum up as if she was on a downhill spiral and was wrong about that too.

The porridge smelled amazing, unlike it should. 'This is delicious, mum. What have you done to it?'

'Sal had a tin of Carnation milk and molasses in the cupboard. I thought that'll put hairs on their chests.'

Viv spluttered her porridge out and Mand ran for a piece of kitchen roll for her and to wipe up the mess she'd fired off her own spoon. The notion that the three of them would aspire to having hairs on their chests was too much for that time of the day. Their mum seemed to have grown in confidence. Had they infantilised her, tucking her away in the Pound? After all it wasn't regarded as God's waiting room for nothing. Looking at the woman standing by the Aga now, erect and strong-limbed, how could they have thought the Pound was a good thing?

James was enjoying his porridge and looked a picture of delight in his unicorn jumper.

Mand spotted her sister staring at James. 'He's a determined wee thing.'

'Not a bad thing. Besides, you must have packed the jumper in the first place.'

'You think. We'd never get out of the house without it. It's one of his security blankets. I made sure there was more than one.'

The difficulties of only having one security blanket wouldn't have occurred to Viv. But what a smart move to have multiples. She'd seen pleas on social media for the return of a favourite this or that bunny, dog, teddy and imagined the chaos of the household until it was returned.

Once they'd had breakfast their mum returned to her room and Viv in a lowered tone said, 'I think you should follow her to church and see what she's up to. I'm guessing she's meeting someone.'

'Why me? I thought I'd give the run a try.'

'Well, how about we both follow her to church and once she's in we can head off to the run. It shouldn't take long to do 5K.'

Mand's face was a picture. 'I haven't run for ages. I'll probably end up walking it.'

'That's all right as long as one of us is there to meet her coming out of church. We'll have just under an hour. She said she'd be at the finish line but she can't be. Even she wouldn't have the balls to walk out of a service before it finished.'

'I'm not so sure. Did you notice how confident she seemed at breakfast?'

Viv nodded. 'I sure did. Whatever she's on I'd love some.'

'Me too.'

'We'd better get a move on if we're to be ready as soon as she comes down.'

Mand held up a large rucksack. 'This is what we need.'

'Wow. We'll only be away for a couple of hours at most.'

'Every eventuality.'

They heard the door of the bedroom upstairs close and Mand put her thumbs up. 'Game on!'

Viv laughed, 'You're enjoying this, aren't you!'

'Better than sitting at home with *Thomas the Tank* or a box set.'

Viv hadn't really thought about the rhythm of Mand's life. More often than not they just rubbed each other up the wrong way.

They decided to walk into the village and were surprised to see signs for the 'Fun Run' as soon as they reached the main street. There was no one around so however well advertised it had been it wasn't going to be busy.

'I think we must be early,' Mand said as she pushed James in a buggy capable of an Everest ascent. Baby and toddler acquisitions could be quite good fun if it included kit like that. They walked past the Catholic Church whose car park was full and continued along the main street.

Half way along their mum stopped and pointed. 'You guys go that way. Follow the arrows. I'll see you at the end.'

Viv said, 'I thought we might be finished before the service so we'll come and meet you.'

Alarm briefly flitted over their mum's face, but she said, 'Sure. You're probably right.'

'Which church are you going to?'

'Ah, good question. It's the Piscie at the end of the village. Take a left at the cross.'

How did she know this? As far as Viv knew she'd never been to Doune. But after the last couple of days, what could she believe about her mum's past?

They parted company and Viv shooed Mand towards the street their mum had pointed to. 'You head on up and I'll follow her. If she does actually go to church I'll be back with you in a few minutes.'

'And if she doesn't?'

'We'll cross that bridge . . .'

She hesitated for a moment, but then complied, so Viv retraced her steps and caught up with Mand in the park where tents and stalls had been erected for registration and a crèche. There were dozens of people milling about shaking out their limbs, checking their Fitbits or sorting their vests. James began to girn as he was taken into the crèche. Viv scanned the pitch and spotted Mac chatting to an official. There were serious athletes as well as locals, who'd obviously joined up for fun since they were in costumes of various superheroes and heroines.

She turned to Mand. 'God only knows what mum's up to. As you say she's an adult. But she's not as young as she was, even if she can beat us at push-ups.'

Mac called, 'Viv' and waved them over. He shook Mand's hand. 'Hi, we probably last met in the street when we were kids.' He handed them vests. 'I've registered your names. Where's your mum?'

'Change of plan. She's found God this morning.'

Mac raised his eyebrows. 'Old school.'

'What d'you mean?'

'Meetings in churches. Churches were known as the office because they were so often used as drop points.'

Viv shook her head, 'She's not exactly Mata frickin' Hari.'

'Don't you believe it. C'mon, we're almost off. Pretend you're doing some stretches or they won't let you run. We're only in for the 5K. Walk in the park.' He winked, did a perfect salute to the sun and touched his toes effortlessly. Viv concentrated on her hamstrings. Mand copied them both.

The elite runners lined up at the front and the gun went off. It was a slow start because of a narrow funnel before the track opened onto a rough, hard, uneven surface. It was turning into a beautiful bright morning and the air was crisp and fresh. With their breath visible ahead of them they started up a steep incline at a gentle trot chatting effortlessly as they went. There was a dense wood to the left, and open views down to the village on their right. At the quarter way post Mac upped his pace. He and Mand, both competitive, took off but Viv wanted to save herself for a sprint finish. She was trailing behind by about 30 metres when another runner came from behind and pushed her. She flew forward onto the ground. 'Ouch! What the fu . . .?' His foot stamped on her calf. 'You bastard!'

The attacker ran on the spot, waving a few runners past. As soon as they were alone he offered Viv a hand to pull her up. She brushed it away. 'Fuck off. What do you think you're playing at?'

He grabbed her by the hair and pulled her up wrapping a huge rough hand over her mouth. He began hauling her backwards into the wood. She punched and kicked, managing once to connect with his face, but he was too strong for more. He was as big as Mac, maybe even broader. Within the next few seconds he'd slapped tape over her mouth and tied her hands behind her back. She managed to get to her feet but the branches of the trees were low and there was very little space to manoeuvre. She tried to head butt him and kicked like a mad woman but she couldn't put her full force behind it since her leg was in agony and she couldn't get completely upright.

Eventually, through gritted teeth, he whispered right into her ear, 'There's no point fighting. Keep your strength for later.' A slight accent, English not his first language.

What did he mean 'later'? What she'd thought was a two-minute fracas was turning into a proper abduction.

Alarm bells began clanging in her head. No one goes for a run carrying gaffer tape and string. This was planned. She tried to turn her head to see him, but he forced her forward. 'You're coming with me.' He pushed her from behind again and she stumbled through the undergrowth. It was steep and heavily mulched with a thick bed of pine needles, which made the climb slow and excruciating.

He didn't speak again until they emerged at the top of the treeline. 'No one will hear us here.' A German accent was easily decipherable now, with his tone at normal level. 'Keep moving. We don't have too far to go.' He kept a grip of her wrists from behind and steered her in the direction he wanted to go. She racked her brain for who he was and what the hell he wanted. How was she to get away when she could hardly put weight on her leg? She stopped suddenly, leaned forward and punched her fists back up into his rib cage. He staggered back winded, but recovered and chased after her as she hobbled over the deep heather. Great place for sheep and deer, but for humans to run, not so much. He rugby tackled her and they both fell to the ground. She kicked and struggled but with only one good leg her options were restricted. She managed to roll on top of him but the only thing she could do was try to head butt him again, and this time she connected in all the right places. He screamed and pushed her over. She scrambled to her feet and tried to kick him but lost her balance. She crawled away from him and got up again. No matter the pain she had to run. She didn't get far. He tackled her again. This time his full weight pinned her to the ground and he spoke into her ear, 'Don't do that again.' The menace in his voice didn't worry her, it just made her angry. The smell of his blood gave her some satisfaction. He gripped her wrists and steered her to just before the edge of the wood, where they descended through the trees. They reached a narrow track with such a steep icy camber that it was difficult to stay upright. He pushed her on. On the opposite side of the track was an apocalyptic landscape of recently felled pines, barren and stubbly with remnants of trunks sticking up, as if an atomic bomb had gone off. He pushed her to the left and then right onto another rough path flanked with gorse bushes. A black pick-up truck had been reversed in. The sound of a PA system echoed in the distance. The runners would be crossing the finish line and Mac and Mand would surely be wondering where the hell she was.

Her mind went into overdrive at the job they would have to find her if she didn't leave enough evidence behind for them to discover. The German pushed her hard and she allowed herself to fall over onto the gorse, snapping a few small branches on her way down. He hauled her up and jabbed her in the back. He would so regret this when she got her hands untied. She dug a deep footprint into a soft area of earth. A few hundred yards on she spotted a mast, probably a mobile phone tower, badly disguised as a tree, but a few metres ahead of it there was a door into what looked like a water tower. It made sense to her that there would be a water collection tank at this height but why would he be interested in it? Her belly began to lurch. If he intended to shove her inside, she'd be a goner in no time. Although the sun was up the temperature still hadn't gone above freezing. She could see his breath in the air. She panicked, yanking her hands free of his grip, and spun round to knee him in the groin but this time he was ready for her and he kicked out at her sore leg. She squealed and squirmed as she hit the ground. As she rolled around on the decking he prised open the iron door and dragged her inside.

To her astonishment it wasn't a water tank at all, but some kind of reinforced concrete bunker, with a path leading down and down into the hill. He banged the door shut and they were engulfed in darkness. She tried to keep her wits about her, paying attention to the smell of dampness and counting her steps to give her an idea of how far she was going. After a while the gradient flattened out and he flipped a switch. Lights flickered on, illuminating the way ahead. The corridor reeled out until eventually they came to another huge reinforced steel door painted in army issue green. It was slightly ajar. She imagined he'd been there already to prepare the way. He shoved her through the gap before struggling to push it closed even with the full weight of his back on it. She winced at it scraping on the concrete, worse than nails on a blackboard. They were now in another corridor, this time with lots of doors off it on either side. Holy shit! From the notices on the doors they had to be in a disused Cold War bunker, 'Dry store', 'Boiler 1', 'Cold store', 'Sanatorium', 'Operations', which may or may not have been of the medical variety. The next door sent a chill up her spine with its yellow skull and crossbones sign and 'Decontamination' written in red letters. He kept pushing her forward until they came to a door marked 'Bunks'. Inside, rows of narrow iron bed frames, with wooden planks where a mattress could be placed, lined either side of walls that had once been whitewashed. Poor lighting made everything grey. It was a massive underground complex of buildings where a chosen few would have come to survive a nuclear attack, designed to keep people safe for weeks, even months. Her mind flitted from one scenario to another. Finding her here would push Mac's limits.

He closed the door of the bunkroom and ripped the gaffer tape off her mouth. She wanted to yelp but wouldn't give him the satisfaction.

'What the fuck do you want with me?'

He shoved her onto a bed. She landed with a thud, her heart pounding with adrenalin. If he thought she'd be an easy lay he was badly mistaken. But to her relief he didn't start to fumble with her joggers or his own jeans. If he wanted to kill her he needn't have gone to all the trouble of hauling her through the woods and bringing her underground. He'd had lots of opportunity before now, so he must have something else in mind.

'You have something that belongs to me.'

She didn't answer straightaway. Her face crumpled in thought, but she shook her head. 'Nope. I've no idea what you mean.'

Viv had had a situation in the recent past where someone believed she had something which belonged to them and it had been a difficult fight. At first she'd thought he might be right, but it turned out that he was as unworthy of the inheritance as she was. She sighed, 'Is this about Dawn?'

The look of confusion that passed over his face made her sure it wasn't.

'Okay, tell me what it is you want.'

'I, we, want what is rightfully ours.'

'I know that you think I've got special powers and can guess what you're on about, but trust me I don't. It would help if you took me through it from the beginning.'

He plonked himself down on the bed opposite, took out a handkerchief and wiped his face. She noticed a slight twitch above his right eye and remembered seeing the same thing on someone recently. The pianist. This man was not the pianist, but they were both German. Could there be a connection? Could a twitch be hereditary? She had nothing to lose, 'Are you related to Kurt Hahn?'

Wrong question.

'Ah, so you do know what I want.'

'No, I don't.'

'Then how would you know of my connection to Kurt?'

'It was a wild guess.'

He snorted. 'You don't strike me as the wild guess type.'

'Well stick around, you'll soon find out how much guessing I can do.'

'I'm not sticking around as you say, but you are not going anywhere for a while.'

'What is this about? What do you think I have belonging to you?'

'Money.'

'Ah, it's always about money. But I don't have your money.'

'You might not have it now, but you will when your mother dies.'

Major alarm bells rang at the mention of her mum. 'So, I'm guessing it's a significant amount of money, otherwise why would you go to this extent to get it back? Not sure why you assumed I'll inherit.' She was about to say everything her mum owned would go to James but stopped herself. The less he knew of James and Mand the better.

He smirked, 'It is a substantial sum.'

'Do you know that she actually has it?' She thought of the receipt squirrelled away in the secret compartment of her mum's box.

He nodded. 'And since we're both guessing, you also know and are playing a game with me. Let's see how you enjoy the game of being locked in here for . . .' He stood and pushed her back onto the hard boards on the bed. He punched her with his full force on the side of the head and she went out cold.

Chapter Eleven

She came round in darkness, frozen and stiff, no feeling in her arms since both her hands were tied above her head to the bed frame. Her temple thumped and her eyes were blurred, but she was alone in the silence. How long had she been unconscious? Would he be back? It was dark, but it would be anyway since the lights were out and there was no natural light. She drew in a breath and thought the smell of his blood lingered. Maybe she had some on her. She moved her legs, pulling her knees up towards her chest. Best keep still, her bladder objected. Interesting that he hadn't tied them to the other end of the bed. He was confident that she wouldn't find a way to release her hands. He was right. The tethers were cutting into her wrists and when she moved the pain was excruciating. The more she moved the more damage she did. She felt blood trickle down her arm. This was bad news. She should lie still and think of a strategy. Mac and Mand would already be looking for her. It was just a matter of time. What time was it? She had a mobile tucked into her pants but she'd switched it to silent for the run. Besides there was no way she could access it. She cursed. Not that that would do any good, but it released some tension. She tried rubbing her wrists up and down the iron bedstead, every movement agonising. She could use her blood as a lubricant, but only when it was flowing. Biting on her lip she continued slow movements up and down the post. It was rough with rust or peeling paint, but to break the ties she would have to commit to a long process. The metallic smell of her blood made her conscious that there were no other smells.

Suddenly she heard a noise. She stopped moving her arms. Silence. She lay holding her breath, then she heard it again, the scraping of the huge door. It wouldn't be long before he came in. It seemed an age until the door to the bunkroom was pushed open. She immediately became aware of a rank stench. Then the lights sprang on. She gasped. But the thing in the doorway screamed. She blinked and blinked as if she was clearing a nightmare from her vision. The apparition before her couldn't be human. It had a mass of matted hair that gave a whole new meaning to dreadlocks, and layers of clothing and ropes tied round its waist and round its ankles. It wore boots that were far too big and it was filthy everywhere. The face looked charred but was probably ingrained with dirt and weather. It had put its hands up to cover its mouth and the black fingernails were long and curling. It started to back out of the door.

'No, wait!' she shouted.

It continued to retreat.

'Please. Don't go. Don't leave me.'

But she heard it continue to shuffle away from the door.

She called out again, 'Please. I can't hurt you.'

Either it had stopped or it was too far away for her to hear its movement.

'Shit! Shit! Shit!'

She glanced around the room and back up at her wrists. What a mess. There was blood everywhere now but the tethers had loosened off slightly. If she kept at it eventually one of them would give. Slow and patient movements would win the day so she began again, holding back tears of frustration as she did. Again she thought she heard shuffling and the apparition stuck its head round the door. This time she made no eye contact and didn't speak. Whoever they were they must be familiar with this place and until now probably believed that they had it to themselves. She risked glancing up. It raised its hands to its face again and turned away.

She said, 'I'm sorry. I'm sorry to be here.'

It fidgeted with the string at its waist. Then shook its head.

'If you help me to free my hands I'll get out of your way . . .'

Its agitation increased when she spoke. She took a deep breath and continued working her wrists on the iron bedstead and ignored the person. What would have had to happen to someone, for them to become like that? She knew she was dealing with a serious mental condition, but was there a way for her to communicate without freaking it out? Her freedom was in both their interests. It occurred to her that there might not be much time. Her attacker could return at any minute then what? This poor human being could also be in danger.

'Who are you?' a croaky but female voice asked.

Viv's belly contracted. The way she handled this could make or break her release. 'My name is Viv. I was running in the race and someone attacked me and brought me here. Can you help me?' She kept her voice low and steady although her nerves were in danger of betraying her.

'I can't help you. But I wish you weren't here. This is my place. No one comes here.'

'I'm sorry . . .'

This immediately sent the woman into a state of agitation again. She started moaning, a low painful rumble, almost a growl, that went straight to Viv's heart. She'd heard it once before and had hoped she'd never hear the like of it again. An undercover job had gone badly wrong and she'd ended up trapped in a container along with a group of women who were intended for sale. One had a daughter who was ill and both were claustrophobic. The mother had made this same noise as she'd rocked her child back and forth, waiting for death. The woman in the room with her now smelled of filth, but mainly of fear.

'I'm injured. He stamped on my leg so that I couldn't run.'

The woman stopped moaning, but turned her face to the opposite wall. Viv had no way of knowing how old she was. All she could tell was that she had a hoarse, but not coarse, Scottish accent, she wasn't very tall and she had pale blue eyes that flitted here, there and everywhere.

'Please.'

The woman turned round and took a small step nearer, but wouldn't make eye contact. Viv didn't say anything more. She waited as tiny step by tiny step the woman came closer. She made a darting movement inside the layers of her clothes, if that's what you could call them, and to Viv's astonishment came forward with an old Swiss army knife. Viv's wide -eyed look scared her and she took a step back.

Viv took a breath and let it out really slowly. The woman stepped closer again. Then in a couple of quick steps she rushed to Viv's wrist and sliced through the tether. She did the same at the other side then held the knife aloft, pointing it at Viv.

Viv's arms collapsed in agony. She tried to shake them out but the cold had rendered them immobile. She swung her legs off the bed. 'Thank you.'

She wasn't sure if her injured leg would carry her but she was determined to try. She crossed the room to the door in a few excruciating unstable strides and went out. She dragged herself up the corridor like a troglodyte until she reached the blast door, which was slightly ajar, and squeezed around it. The long corridor ahead felt steeper than it had on the way in but she reached the exit and emerged blinking into dark, cool, fresh air. As she reached the rough path with the gorse on either side she heard the drone of an engine. She slipped into the wood at the other side of the track and wound her way downhill where she could see the lights of the village. The truck passed by but she didn't try to see who the driver was. She just needed to find her way home. Only fifty metres on she heard a movement behind her. She froze and turned as Molly appeared through the undergrowth and started circling her legs and jumping up at her. She barked but Viv got onto the ground with her and held her muzzle to silence her. Tears sprang to her eyes as she rubbed the dog's ears. More than relieved to see her. Mac and Mand must be out on the hill looking for her. She sat with the dog until the engine noise vanished. Then she hobbled to her feet and continued the descent.

She heard Mac's voice calling on the dog and felt safe to call back, 'Over here! I've got Moll.'

Within a couple of minutes Mac came into sight. He raced to her and held her in a bear hug. He spoke into her hair, 'What . . .'

She pulled away. 'Not here.'

'Christ, Viv, I thought I'd lost you.' He choked.

She held him again. Both tried to disguise tears of relief. 'I'll be okay but my leg is in a bad way.'

He scooped her up and carried her down the track, Molly jumping and circling with excitement all the way. His Audi was parked on the other side of the park, where all trace of the running event and PA system had disappeared. He managed to carry her all the way.

Once inside the car he noticed the blood on her arms and the mess her wrists were in, 'My God, what the hell happened out there?'

'Let's get home. Where's Mand?'

He shook his head, 'What a day. Home.'

It only took a couple of minutes to get to the cottage. The porch light was on and with a few of the rooms also lit up it looked cosy and homely. He came round to her side of the car, intending to carry her in, but she shooed him away. 'I'll be fine now. Don't fuss.'

'Oh, there's going to be fussing.'

She picked up something in his tone. 'What kind of fussing?'

He opened the front door and ushered her in.

Chapter Twelve

Mand rushed over and hugged her. 'My God, what happened to you?'

Viv, overwhelmed by Mand's emotional response, said, 'I'd love to get cleaned up a bit before I . . . Where's mum?'

Mand shot a look at Mac.

'Where is she?'

Mac said, 'She didn't come back from church.'

'Who have you contacted?'

'I've put out an alert, a description with the local force, but we can't confirm her as a missing person until twenty-four hours have passed.'

Viv opened her mouth to object, then decided against. 'Ten minutes.' She hobbled upstairs and ran the shower.

Mand said, 'Well, that went well.'

Mac said, 'Better than I expected, but now she's got thinking time we should prepare for war.'

Mand shook her head, 'Is she really that bad?'

Mac looked confused. 'She's not at all bad. In fact, she's the best we have.'

It was Mand's turn to look confused. 'What do you mean "the best we have"? It sounds as if she's working for you.'

He shrugged. Viv's secrets were not his to tell. 'Let's just say she's an extraordinary woman.'

'I can't get my head round any of this cloak and dagger shit. A couple of days ago I had a sister who was a brainy hairdresser and a mum in a retirement home. We are, were, a dysfunctional family who ticked along. If the chips were ever really down we could rely on one another, but now, I've no idea who they are or where I stand.'

The sound of the shower pumping water stopped. Mand put the kettle on the Aga. A few minutes later Viv appeared wearing a long baggy tee shirt and carrying a first aid box. She plonked herself down on a chair at the kitchen table and opened the box. Sal hadn't held back. Anything could be fixed by its contents. Mac sat beside her and checked her wrists. Now that they were clean he could see how deeply she'd been cut.

'Ouch! These should be stitched.' He rifled around in the box and found butterflies in a selection of sizes. 'These will do as a temporary measure.' He was gentle and dextrous and in no time her wrists were bandaged. Then he turned his attention to her leg. Her knee was grazed, gravel still obvious in it. He set about removing bits with tweezers. She wasn't brave about this and had to look elsewhere as he poked and prodded. Her calf was badly swollen but she could move it in every direction he asked her to. 'I don't think it's broken, do you?'

'No. But it's bloody painful to put weight on it.'

He put a dressing on her knee and lashings of arnica gel on her calf and shin. 'Let's get a look at your head.'

'My head's fine . . . thank you.' She hobbled back upstairs and returned wearing joggers and thick socks. 'Now let's talk about mum.'

'We'll get to that, but first I'd like to hear exactly what happened up that hill.'

His face told her that she wasn't getting any info until she spilled her story.

'Okay. Just before the bend after the steep quarter-way mark a man came up behind me and shoved me to the ground. At first I thought it was an overzealous runner trying to get past but he wasn't. Once I was on the ground he waited until a gap in the runners and he stamped on my leg then dragged me into the wood.' She closed her eyes, 'Christ, it sounds so dramatic. Anyway, he managed to get my hands tethered behind my back, which made it easy for him to push, and at times drag me up through the forest. Long story short . . .'

'No! Not short. I'd prefer the whole story.' He was wearing his stern I'm-having-no-nonsense face.

She sighed and continued. 'Okay. We reached the end of the wood which was pretty high up on the Braes. Probably at the same latitude as your place.'

'Nice detail, but go on and keep on track. All this could be important if we're going to find your mum.'

'We had a few scuffles but he overwhelmed me with his weight.' She flushed. Embarrassed.

'Don't worry about that. You managed to outsmart him, otherwise you wouldn't be here.'

'I didn't. He took me to an old bunker. Massive place underground. He tied me to a rusty iron bunk. Thus the welts.' She lifted her wrists. 'He punched me in the side of the head. And I went out.'

Mand gasped and fought back tears. 'I can't cope. What if someone is doing the same thing with mum?'

Mac said, 'Let's hear what Viv has to say first, then we'll get to your mum.'

Viv swallowed, then continued. 'When I came round the place was in darkness and he had gone. But the weirdest, and I mean weirdest thing happened.'

Mac nodded to urge her on.

'A woman, not like any woman I've seen before came into the bunker. She obviously uses it as her shelter, because she screamed and screamed when she saw me. She's not well, but after a while I persuaded her to cut me free. We should find her; she needs help. She was terrified.'

'She might well need help, but she was doing all right until you interrupted her day and will probably live to see another in the bunker.'

'The rest you know. I got out and into the wood. I heard a truck going up the track and thought it might be him returning. I hid and that's when Moll found me. I was worried when she barked that if it was him he might hear her and come looking. Irrational. Even if it had been him he wouldn't necessarily have heard her bark and certainly wouldn't have thought it was because of me. I wasn't thinking straight.' She covered her face with her hands, but winced when she caught the side of her head.

Moll came out from her bed and curled up on top of her feet.

'Now what are we going to do about mum?'

'I'll get the local guys to search the bunker. They're supposed to be locked up, inaccessible.'

'So you knew it was there.'

'All government officials know it's there.'

'But you're not . . .'

He shook his head. 'Need to know only.'

'Don't scare that poor woman. If that's her only place to sleep in the cold . . .'

'I'm on it, Viv.' He wandered off with his mobile phone pinned to his ear.

Mand put a mug of coffee down in front of her sister. 'Here, drink this.'

'Thanks. How's James?'

'He's finally gone off to sleep. Probably not for long though, too much excitement.'

Viv checked the clock. Then walked through to the conservatory and leafed through a magazine rack. She pulled out a local monthly publication about village news. On the back page she read the times of each of the local church services. If she was quick she'd catch the rector after Evensong. She grabbed her car key and was half way into her jacket when Mac came in from the porch and saw her getting ready to go out. 'Where are you off to?'

'Church. There's an Evensong about to finish. I'll ask the rector about mum. Can't sit here doing nothing. Coming?'

Mand said, 'What about me?'

'You've got James to look after. I don't expect we'll be very long and if we are more than, say half an hour, I'll phone you.'

Mand didn't look happy but seemed resigned to stay put. Mac and Viv left.

Mac said, 'I'll drive. You save that leg while you can.'

She didn't argue and hoisted herself into the Audi.

They drove to the small but perfectly formed church and waited. Soon the doors opened and the congregation began to spill out. When it seemed as if everyone had gone they went inside. Viv saw the rector disappear through a small heavy wooden door. She wandered up the aisle and knocked on the door, which was duly opened by the woman in the midst of her de-robing.

'Sorry to trouble you, but we're looking for my mum.'

The rector held the door wide open and smiled. 'Well, she's not in here.'

'No, I didn't think she would be. She was here this morning and didn't come home.' It occurred to her that her mum could still be in the building. 'Is there another door?'

She pointed to a curtain and pulled it back to expose a narrow wooden door. 'The loo is in there and it also has a door leading outside.'

Viv went through to the loo and out the other door into the garden and the car park. No sign of her mum.

The rector had followed. 'There was a woman here who left before Eucharist.'

Viv asked, 'Was she wearing a camel coloured coat?'

The rector shrugged, 'I couldn't say for sure. But she was with someone.'

Mac joined them. 'Can you describe them?'

The rector drew herself up and breathed out a sigh. 'Am I about to get someone into trouble?'

'No, no, but she could be in danger.'

'What kind of danger?'

Viv shook her head. 'We're not sure. There's been someone following her.'

Mac said, 'You never said.'

'Who was she with? Male or female?'

'Male. They looked as if they knew each other but I could be wrong. The only reason I noticed was they were both strangers to the congregation.'

'Shit!' Viv glanced at the rector who shrugged again and said, 'I don't think I can give you any more help.'

'Wait, what time was the Eucharist?'

The rector glanced at her watch, a habitual gesture. 'At ten twenty.'

'So the last sighting of her was . . . eight hours ago. She's been on the move for more than eight hours.'

'Viv, she could be anywhere.'

She said, 'This is so out of character.'

Mac said, 'But is it? Is it out of character now that you know that she's had a different life to the one you thought she'd had?'

'How the hell would I know? She's become a loose cannon. We should go home and check through her things.'

Mac stood with his hands on his hips and stared at her.

'What?' Viv said, irritably. 'Basics. We've got to start with basics. If she's not come home then we'll think of plan B. But what did he look like?' she called to the rector's retreating back.

The rector turned. 'Tweeds, ruddy complexion, smiling eyes.'

Viv looked at Mac and screwed up her eyes. 'Are you thinking what I'm thinking?'

'Could be Ruddy?'

'What the hell? That would be confusing, weird even. I mean she doesn't know him.'

Mac said, 'You don't know that. You've no idea what connections she's had or still has. If she wasn't your mum you'd be thinking totally differently.'

'You're right. I have to try to see this as some woman with a past . . . C'mon, let's get back and check the house.'

They drove back to be greeted by an excitable Moll twirling like a Dervish in the hallway.

Mand said, 'I have to have a shower. Can you listen out for James?'

Viv was distracted so Mac replied, 'Sure, go for it.'

Mand nodded gratefully.

Mac took his phone out and began texting,

Viv noticed. 'What are you doing?'

'I'm sending the big boss a message.'

She said, 'D'you think he knows her?'

He shrugged, 'Only one way to find out.'

'She must have a phone. There's no way that she arranged this before we came because she didn't know she was coming until Mand persuaded her.'

Mac raised his eyebrows. 'You think?'

'Will you stop doing that?'

'Well, you'll have to do better, 'cause you're not thinking straight. So let's start from the beginning. Or at least from what information we've got.'

Viv sighed. 'Right. She has a visitor in the shape of a window cleaner who turns out not to be a window cleaner but a petty thief. Mand sees her hiding a paper in a box with a secret compartment so we go and check it out. We discover the paper is a document marked top secret and there's a receipt stapled to a photograph. We don't know who the man is, but as you pointed out there was some kind of old military facility in the background. Mand was followed.'

'What here, since she came to the village?'

Viv nodded, 'It gets worse. The man, well we think it was the same man, then came into the garden and mum spotted him and went out to ask him what he wanted. He took off and so did she. Tried to catch him but he waded over the river. Thankfully she didn't and I found her on her way back.'

'Wow. So things are stacking up.'

'Then she showed us a bag that she'd brought with her. She didn't think it was safe at her flat. In fact it should be upstairs.'

Viv went up to find the tapestry bag. It wasn't there. How could that be? Her mum hadn't taken it with her to church. Had she been back to collect it? Viv checked beneath the bed, in the wardrobe, then noticed a hatch in the ceiling. No way! She started to pull the chest of drawers away from the wall.

Mac stuck his head round the door. 'What on earth are you . . .'

'What does it look like? I can't find the bag and she didn't take it with her. She pointed to the hatch and started to haul herself onto the dresser.

She said, 'Lift me up and I'll be able to grab it.'

Mac stepped forward, lifted her off the drawers and dumped her on the bed. 'I don't think so.' He stood on the drawers and sure enough when he pushed open the hatch the bag was there. He hauled it out.

She said, 'My God, this is like some mad country house mystery. How the hell did she get it up there?'

Mac stared at her and nodded at the chest sitting in the middle of the floor. 'No prizes!' He shoved it back to where it had been. 'Let's have a look. There's bound to be something in there that'll help.'

They sat side by side on the bed. It had been made with military precision;

her mum would do nothing less if she were at home. They carefully pulled envelopes and papers from the bag. Mac slipped the photographs of her dad out of their envelope but didn't say anything. She kept her eyes fixed on the documents her mother had been saving for another time. Each yellowed sheet was marked with the same 'Top Secret' stamp as the one they'd found in the box back in Edinburgh. 'Interesting that she's separated these from the one in the box at home. In fact, surely it's here. It was well hidden so it is important to her.'

Mac glanced at Viv's pile. 'D'you think she's keeping those for posterity? I mean they must be of great sentimental value. And probably not of any consequence to anyone else apart from for her.'

Viv handed each one to him after she'd glanced over it. They were all addressed to her mum but had words blacked out. Only one was addressed to her dad. 'D'you think she was trying to hide this one? You know, place it somewhere so obvious that no one would find it?'

'Could be. Let's have a look.'

She passed it over. The date on it was 1989. The documents addressed to her mum were mostly dated in the late nineteen seventies, before Mand and Viv were born.

Mand stepped into the room, rubbing her hair with a towel. 'What are you doing?'

'As you see. We're trying to find something that will help us to find her.'

'But she hasn't been away for long. She's probably having a dinner somewhere and we're getting totally worked up over nothing. And you're prying into her private papers. She said she wasn't going to show us those.'

Mac nudged Viv's arm. 'Look at this.' He handed her one of the sheets of paper addressed to her mum.

It read: **'You are summoned to attend Special Training School 24, Group A, at Arisaig in September and October where you will receive intensive instruction in fieldcraft, night and daylight navigation, weapons and demolition. Etcetera.'**

The date at the top of the letter was barely visible. She thought it could be August 1971 but it was too faded.

Mac said, 'Believe me now?'

Viv fingered the side of her head and glanced at Mand whose eyes were welling up and said, 'Okay we'll just put everything back for now.'

Mand's voice was soft, 'The damage is done. But she could walk in the door any minute and you'd have to explain what you're up to.'

'Look, Mand, we're not "up to" anything other than trying to make sure she isn't hurt. I'd love her to walk in the door right now, but my gut tells me she isn't going to. She's up to something and probably out of her depth.'

Viv packed everything into the bag and with Mac's help dragged the chest of drawers back over to where he could reach the hatch. Mac jumped up and lifted the bag back into position.

Viv said firmly, 'If she doesn't turn up by morning we'll go out and look for her. Someone is bound to have noticed her. She's a stranger in a small village. Meantime I'll contact . . .' she glanced at Mac, 'You haven't heard back?'

He said, 'No, nothing. And we don't actually know that it was him with her. Lots of people could answer to that description, especially in the countryside. Let's get food and discuss a strategy for tomorrow.'

They traipsed downstairs. Mand looked vulnerable with limp damp hair and no makeup. James stirred and she went to see him. Was he aware of the rising tension around him?

Mac set about preparing food. He was an exceptional cook. His Italian heritage came to the fore in the kitchen. Mand appeared with a whimpering James pinned to her hip. A sleepy wee boy caught in the middle of a family drama. They sat round the kitchen table and ate, then discussed what should happen next. Viv was all for setting out on foot but the other two protested.

Mac said, 'Does she have a mobile phone?'

Viv shrugged. 'I think she must have, but I've never seen it. She organised the meeting in the church while she was here and the only way she could do that would be on a mobile. But I'm surprised that Mand and I didn't see or hear her using it.'

'You might be underestimating her. If she has a plan she could be leading you two a merry dance.'

The sisters were about to protest in unison but Mac raised his hand. 'She has had a life that you know nothing about. From that letter I showed you I think she's been a well-trained operative and you are blind to her skills because she's your mum. C'mon, Viv, imagine if she was anyone else. What would you do?'

'If she was anyone else I wouldn't be this worried. And the key word in that last sentence is "been", past tense, a previous life. She's seventy, for God's sake.'

'My point exactly. Your concern is getting in the way of your reason.'

'If you say that once more I'll . . .' She heaved a sigh, ' . . . How much CCTV do you think Doune has?'

'Enough. And if you concentrate you'll recall from your own training . . .'

Viv glared at him. Mand had no clue about Viv's training. But now that he mentioned it Mand said, 'Well? What training is that?'

'Nothing that you need to know about.'

'Not unless it puts me or James in danger.'

'It won't.' Viv was lying; it already had once before and there were no guarantees that it wouldn't again. Although she'd go to any lengths to prevent it. Already people, whoever these people were, had shown up not worried about being visible. They knew too much about her and her family. She reached for her laptop.

'What are you going to do?'

'I'm going to check the CCTV situation.'

Mac said, 'D'you mind if I have a shower and pretend that I know nothing about what you're up to?'

'Go ahead. D'you know where to find a towel?'

He nodded and glanced at Mand. 'You okay?'

'What are my choices?'

'Your sis is pretty switched on in the computer department.'

'You don't say.'

'Oh and by the way, we can't exclude the idea that your mum could be shacked up in a hotel room getting some action with an old flame.' He grinned, but on watching their looks of revulsion, and both reaching for a missile, he took off upstairs.

Viv said, 'Sod! That image once seen can never be unseen. He's disgusting. How could he?'

Mand said, 'I don't know about you, but I'm not getting the hang of this. In my head, as I said earlier, our mum's a retired secretary who settled into sheltered accommodation to be entertained in her retirement. She isn't someone who'd go bouncing around . . . the countryside.'

'Don't pay any attention to him. He's just winding me up. By the way how did you persuade her to come?'

'I had a vague idea where Sal lived and for some reason knew the name of the house. When I told mum that seemed to clinch the deal. In the end she was quite keen to come to Perthshire. Now that I think of it she might have said she was fond of Perthshire.'

'That could be important. Can you remember exactly what she said?'

Mand rubbed her hands over her face and into her hair in the same way that Viv often did. It was a habit they'd inherited from their mum. 'Yes, she did say she was fond of Perthshire. It didn't occur to me to ask if she'd been before. If you'd been staying somewhere else I wonder if she'd have stayed at home?'

'So maybe there's a reason, a specific reason for her to come here.'

Viv grabbed her laptop and went upstairs. She'd have to take another look at those old documents.

Mac stepped out of the bathroom with one towel wrapped round his waist and another in his hand rubbing his hair.

Viv averted her eyes. He was in terrific shape. She said, 'I need time out.' She shut her bedroom door and lay prone on the bed. The emotional toll of spending time with the family was beginning to chalk up and what was Mac thinking walking about out there almost naked? She read a return text from Ruddy. He was out of the country unable to help and clearly not the man that her mum had just met, unless he was lying.

She sent a text to Sal. She checked the time. Sal's day would just be starting. No such thing as a weekend off with the FBI. She hoped she'd hear back immediately, but nothing happened. She guessed texts and emails were monitored but still she ought to have heard something by now even if they had been delayed on some data collection server for Homeland Security. She was under no illusion that Sal's communication would be vetted.

The other possibility, that she didn't want to entertain, was that Sal was too busy enjoying her new job to respond. She booted up her laptop. There had to be a way of checking the CCTV. After a few blind alleys she did manage to hack into the right system, but the broadband kept cutting out and buffering. If her mum wanted to take risks who was she to prevent her? Mand was right; she was an adult. However, she did want to find out what the heck was going on and that meant taking another look inside her room. Her mum having a mobile seemed inevitable but ran counter to her phobia of telephones and any communication over the wire.

She must have fallen asleep and woke with a start. She was cold and stiff again, but she was safe. The bedroom lamp was still on and her laptop lay at her side. She checked the time, two-thirty, middle of the night. She switched the lamp off, pulled the duvet over her and tried to settle back to sleep. Her head flooded with images of that poor woman. What had happened to her? How did she survive in freezing temperatures? The locals must know her or at least have seen her. She felt sick at the thought of the German finding her, but Mac said he was on it. She'd have to trust him for now.

Chapter Thirteen

Monday

At breakfast the following morning Mand and James were eating porridge and Mac was hovering over the Aga waiting for bread to toast. He said, 'Sleep okay?'

'Not bad. How come you're here so early?' She didn't wait for an answer. 'I'm worried about that woman. Hello, wee James.' She rubbed the top of his head.

Mac said, 'Don't be worried. Social services know her. She's with them now. Apparently every few months they take her in and clean her up, but she always goes back out to wander. Can't stand other people.'

'And mum, anything?'

'Nothing. But they think they have a partial registration number of a pick-up that was up there last night.'

'So you've spoken to them already this morning?'

He touched the side of his nose, 'You don't know the extent of my powers.'

She snorted. In that kind of mood, she'd get very little sense from him. Better let him eat. She poured herself a coffee from the pot and slouched into a chair at the table. Her arms ached, her head thumped and her leg was throbbing. 'My only consolation is that I don't think he, or they, want to kill her. There'd be no point when they want something they believe she has. They need her alive.'

'What exactly did he say to you?'

'He said that he wanted money back that belongs to him. He believes that mum has it and that we'll inherit it . . .'

She left that hanging for a minute. 'So maybe . . .'

Mand said, 'No, don't say that. That would mean he intends to . . .' She stifled whatever she was going to say next and buried her face in James' hair.

Mac said, 'They are searching for the pick-up. Soon as we get positive . . . '

Viv interrupted, 'He surely can't have gone far. He won't go away unless he gets what he came for. And for that he needs mum or us. Can we access the bunker?'

Mac nodded, 'Yes. Most of the rooms will be locked, but I'll do my best to get keys.'

'How did he know about the bunker? Could that just have been chance? Or does he have a connection?'

She thought of the photographs with military huts in the background. 'Think Viv, think,' she whispered.

'If we get those photographs out again we can have them enhanced. See if anything more shows up that might identify where they were taken and who the man was.'

Viv pushed her chair back, but Mac stopped her.

'Breakfast first.'

'God, you're so bossy.'

Mand shook her head, 'You two should get a room. You're like a . . .'

Viv said, 'Spare me. Don't even go there.'

Mac smiled, 'It's a love hate thing, but mostly . . .'

Mand said, 'I'm not daft. There's very little hate going on in this room.'

Mac put a rack of toast on the table and handed Viv a plate.

Mand smiled, 'I rest my case.'

Viv said, 'By the way what do you think the "Etcetera" at the end of that letter meant?'

Mac shrugged, 'Not sure, but I know a man who will.'

'We should go through all her correspondence again. See what she was actually being called to do. Something's bound to come to light.'

Mand shook her head. 'I'm not happy. I feel bad about going through her personal papers.'.

'Even if it means they could save a life?'

'Don't you think you're being melodramatic?'

'No, I don't. If you don't want to be around when we do this that's fine.'

'I have to go back to Edinburgh anyway. James has an appointment with the nurse.'

Viv gave her a questioning look, but she didn't elaborate. 'Fair enough. But you'll come back here after it?'

Mand shrugged, 'I wasn't planning to.'

Mac said, 'Probably best to keep you all under one roof. Makes it easier to look out for you.'

Mand didn't answer, just pushed her chair back and took James upstairs. 'I'll go get him ready.'

Once she was out of earshot Viv said, 'D'you think it's safe for her to go?'

'How would I know? But I'd like to see you try and stop her. I'll call in her registration number; get someone on her tail.'

'Thanks. As soon as she goes we'll get that bag down and go through it line by line.'

'I thought you'd want to go back to the bunker. The forecast is for snow later.'

'Okay, bunker first, papers after. Sound like a plan?'

'Sure.'

The drive back up the hill, past the wood and parking where the pick-up had been didn't have much of an effect on her. Mac handed her plastic gloves and bootees. She hunkered down to check the tyre tread marks, scouring the ground around to see if anything had been left behind, but because it had been so cold the ground was rock hard and indentations were minimal. The descent into the bunker, now a crime scene, along the concrete corridor made her belly contract and her mouth dry up. She wondered how he'd reacted when he realised she'd escaped. Then it occurred to her that he might not know. He might have left her there to rot. It wasn't safe to assume that pick-up that she heard last night had been him. There were a couple of farms up on the Braes; it could have been someone going to them.

She said, 'He might not know that I've managed to escape. Wherever he is now he might be imagining me freezing to death down here.'

Mac nodded. 'We should try and question your woman. The guys who picked her up said she was in no state for anything but a bath and a good meal.'

'We could try but I don't think we'd get much out of her. She was definitely a woman of few words.'

'Worth a go, though.'

'Sure. What should we do first, the papers or find the woman? You think she'll still be with social services?'

He shrugged. 'They'd have no way of keeping her against her will. I'll make a call.'

They reached the room where Viv had been kept. Mac pushed the door open with one fingertip, careful not to touch anything. Her attacker's prints would be everywhere; he hadn't worn gloves. She felt her anger rise and pushed it away with long slow breaths. She thought of where her mum might be. Could he have dealt with Viv then found her mum? If he hadn't mentioned that her mum had money belonging to him she'd have believed that the two incidents could be separate. But he had, so the connection was real.

Viv wandered out of the bunkroom, and tried the next door. It was locked. She tried the next and the next until the fifth door opened. From the smell coming from inside she knew that the woman had been in there. Plastic bags filled with plastic bags covered all available floor space, a couple of huge duvets with filthy covers and a load of blankets, some woollen, some fleece, lay over in one corner. A mark on the concrete floor indicated where a hot pot had been laid down. She must have had a camping stove or some way of heating food and water. Viv sighed, concerned about the desperation of the woman. To choose to live like this the poor creature had to believe there were no other possibilities. Living down there was like living in a cave but without the threat of wild animals. Then Viv's presence had terrified her, threatened her safe space. She rubbed her eyes to rid herself of the vision of the woman screaming.

Mac came in behind her. 'Wow. Not exactly homely.'

Viv said, 'Can we get her proper help?'

'Only if she wants it. It's the old story; you can lead a horse to water and all that. Come on, let's get back to the house and go through the papers.'

'She saved my life.'

'You think I'd have given up?'

She stared at him. 'No, I don't suppose you would have.' She took his arm and they made their way outside, both blinking to adjust their eyes to the daylight.

Back at the cottage Mand's car had gone, but there was another in its place. Mac parked and Ruddy extricated himself from the passenger seat of the dark saloon.

Mac said, 'To what do we owe this pleasure? It must be serious to bring you here at this hour of the day.'

Ruddy replied, 'You know the form. Family first.'

Viv cracked, 'I didn't think I qualified as family.'

Ruddy stared at her.

Something in his look. She might be family, but her mum had put in more time.

Mac filled the silence. 'Let's go inside.'

She put the kettle on.

Ruddy gestured at her wrists. 'Painful?'

Mac responded, 'He made sure she was well secured.'

Ruddy slowly nodded his head.

Viv said quickly, 'Mac, can you make coffee and I'll go up and get the bag?'

'Eh, I don't think so. How about you stick to coffee making and I'll get the bag?' It wasn't really a question.

Mac returned and hoisted the bag onto the kitchen table.

Ruddy raised his eyebrows. 'She a hoarder?'

Mac nodded, 'Not too much, but enough to be interesting.' He pulled papers and photographs from the bag.

Ruddy stiffened and stared at the large picture with Viv's mum and the woman in prison issue uniform. He tapped it with the tip of his thick forefinger. 'Cul . . .'

Viv put mugs of coffee on the table. 'What's that?'

His head gave an almost imperceptible shake, but he said, 'Not far.'

She persisted, 'What is it?'

Ruddy said, 'Oh was, all sorts of things. A POW camp mainly disused after World War 2.'

'Mainly, but not entirely?'

He shrugged. 'As soon as one war was over another began. Civilians thought that everything was finished, closed down, after VE day, but it wasn't like that at all. A whole new threat had emerged.'

Viv and Mac waited for him to continue, but he didn't.

Mac said, 'The Cold War?'

Ruddy nodded. 'It took until the late fifties for camps like Culty to have their World War 2 ordnance decommissioned and then it was only because there were accidents. A child killed; a man and his son blown up. Only one survived but he lost an arm. Piles of ammo all over the country, and nowhere to put it. There seemed no point in keeping bullets, grenades and the like, since a completely different kind of danger was looming. Every nation wanted the latest tech. No one cared what happened to a few hundred boxes of grenades. What damage could they do compared to the H-bomb?'

'What does any of this have to do with my mum?'

He scratched his head. 'I'm not sure yet, but she contacted us about five years ago. She'd never done that before so we paid attention.'

'Okay.' Viv rubbed her face in frustration. 'Who's "we" and to what did you pay attention?'

Ruddy looked at her full in the face. 'It shouldn't have become a thing. We'd sorted it. But now I'm not so sure.'

'This "thing", could it endanger her life?'

Ruddy said, 'Let's talk about what happened to you first.'

Viv sighed, but knew he wouldn't take no for an answer. 'I was attacked up on the hill and dragged to a bunker.'

He raised his eyebrows and glanced at Mac, but nodded at Viv to continue.

'So the guy who grabbed me tied me to a bunk and left me unconscious. Luckily for me a woman came and cut me loose. The man has a German accent and a twitch beneath his right eye. It reminded me of another German I met only this week. A pianist who had been asking questions about me. He also had a twitch in the same place. Family tic; do families have tics? I don't know, but it seemed too much of a coincidence. Anyway, my attacker thinks that my mum has money, a substantial amount of money that belongs to him, or he believes is rightly his. And clearly he's making an effort to get it back. My only consolation is that he knows he'll only get it back soon if she's alive. She doesn't have it. I know she doesn't.'

Mac said, 'How can you be sure?'

'Because I've seen the receipt.'

She went to the tapestry bag and rooted around. 'It seems odd that she'd leave it in Edinburgh and bring the rest of this stuff with her. It's got to be in here somewhere.'

'She's a wise woman, Viv. If she left it she'll have had reason to.'

She pointed to the photograph lying on the table in front of Ruddy. 'Who is she? What's her connection to the two Germans?'

'Their mother probably, but without checking her file I can't say for sure.'

'And my mum's connection to her?'

Ruddy began to flick his nails.

Mac said, 'There'll be some clue in here.' He took out more papers and began to leaf through them. 'Viv, you take these and see what you come up with.'

Ruddy pushed his chair back from the table. 'I'll leave you to it. I might be able to find a number somewhere.'

'What kind of number?' Viv was curious.

'A mission number. There could be more than one. I'll keep you posted and you do the same. You've both got my emergency line.'

Viv and Mac nodded as Ruddy walked to the door. He paused. 'I don't think she'll be in any danger. She knows what to do.'

Viv said quietly, 'I wish I were so confident.'

Ruddy sounded quite kindly. 'You should give her some credit.'

Viv snorted, 'For what? I'd no idea until this week that I had a spy for a mother.'

He said, 'Mac, have you got a minute?' They closed the door quietly as they went out.

When Mac returned Viv asked, 'What was that about?'

'Oh nothing, there's stuff going on at HQ.'

'Is it to do with your boss who "left"?'

'God, no. Once you've gone you've gone. His department had already started cleaning up before he cleared his desk.'

'So what is it?'

'The NTF have always been guests at Fettes. Now Police Scotland want more input from us to their other departments.'

'And there's a problem with that kind of sharing caring stuff.' She smiled. 'You can bluff it. Give them a little bit of this and a little bit of that to keep them happy.'

He shook his head. 'Don't know why you don't run my department.'

'Never mind that boring office shit. Tell me you don't think all this is weird, I mean really weird. He,' she pointed to the door as if Ruddy were still there, 'doesn't need to be involved in a family drama.'

'Like the boss said, once in the "family" always in the "family".'

'Oh, for fuck sake, you sound like a character from a 1960s thriller.'

They sat in silence as they read through the papers. Viv made notes and sighed a lot. Her mum had been flown to Berlin and back in a single day more than once. What was she doing there? Why her? Her mum must have been chosen for a reason. She handed a sheet to Mac. 'Why do you think they wanted her for this one? From what I can make out most of her trips were on UK soil.'

His eyes flitted across the document. 'The date on this is obscure. I bet if we can get it under an x-ray we'll find the exact date. Unless of course this is the mission that Ruddy was talking about. He'll get back to us as soon as he finds out but meantime why don't you and I take a look . . .'

His phone rang and he checked the screen. 'I'll take this.' He wandered out to the porch.

She wondered if it was just a privacy habit, or if he thought he got a better signal out of doors. Her own phone buzzed; the arrival of a text from an unknown number. She hoped it would be Sal. It wasn't. She stared in horror at a video of her mum holding up a copy of the *Scotsman*. Her hands were tied in front of her and she spoke slowly, directly to the camera. Viv opened up her laptop and clicked on her email. She had to view this on a bigger screen.

Her mum's voice sounded strong, 'Listen carefully, Vivian. I want you to transfer some money. There's an account book in my bureau. Both you and Mand are named on it so can access the money. Please transfer £500,000 to a sports bag in used ten pound notes . . . one swallow doesn't . . .' The recording was terminated.

When Mac came in, her eyes were glued to the screen. She gestured with her hand to him to come quickly. She wanted to make sure that her mum hadn't been hurt. She replayed it. The video was shaky but she couldn't see any sign that there had been violence. If you were going to have your hands tied, having them in front of you was an easier option than above the head. She touched her own wrists, still tender, and reminded herself that the way her mum looked was staged for the video.

'We have to get this enhanced. I mean I can do it but not to the same degree that your digi guys can. It would help if we could see a bit more of the background. It looks a lot like the bunker, although the lighting's definitely brighter and the chair, look at the edge of the chair back, it's more modern than anything . . . She can't be up there . . .'

Mac said, 'It's a big facility. It isn't impossible.'

'But I thought you'd had it searched?'

'I asked the local guys to do it, but they probably have no idea just how extensive the place is. One room leads to another and another. It's a maze. I'll get on to them again. But that call I had, they think they've spotted the pick-up on a back road to Braco.'

'So no other sightings in the village here?' She gestured with her hand toward the Braes. 'I'll have to go to Edinburgh and get the account book.'

'Ring Mand and get her to pick it up. But there's no way you should make a transfer. Let me send that video on to the right person before we do anything else. I'll send a copy to the boss. He might notice something.'

'Oh my God, I can't think straight. What is wrong with me?' She marched off and rang Mand. No answer. She left a message on her voicemail. 'What now? I'd like to go back up to the bunker and have a proper look. Were they all built to the same spec?'

'There were different grades. Some were built for use for longer periods. There are lots and lots of them. In fact if I remember correctly, one within every fifteen-mile radius over Scotland.'

'Wow! That's a lot of concrete.'

'Some are small radio facilities. There are only half a dozen of the civil . . .'

'Civil what? You don't have to hold anything back from me. I've also signed the OSA remember . . . Let's look at a map.' She got her laptop. 'You said Braco was the last sighting of the pick-up?'

He shook his head. 'Not that kind of map. There are maps still under wraps with the facilities marked on.'

She clicked on the keys and found another map as he described. 'This kind of thing, from the Royal Ordnance Corps?'

'Well, since it's in the public domain it won't be accurate. I'm talking about secret MOD maps.'

'Are you saying that these maps,' she pointed to the screen, 'have misinformation on them?'

He nodded, 'Yep. Don't imagine fake news is a recent development. The Cecils were masters of it in the sixteenth century. I'm amazed that people believe anything that they read or hear in the news. It's all propaganda.'

She shot him a quizzical look.

'Do you know that recently an archaeologist applied to dig an area, because he'd "checked" the maps and believed it was MOD free, but it wasn't. Think about it, Viv, it wasn't in our interests to have accurate maps out there for these facilities.'

'But someone knows the actual positions?'

He nodded.

She checked Google Maps again and traced her finger from Doune to

Braco. It wasn't far at all. 'He must have somewhere to stay. Maybe he's using the pick-up or the bunker.' She was thinking out loud.

Mac hesitated. 'I've . . .'

She caught something anxious in his tone, 'What? Got to be somewhere?'

She didn't expect him to say yes, but he did.

'I should be . . .'

She snapped, 'Don't let me keep you back.'

'I've been trying to cancel stuff, but I can't get hold of one person.'

'And you have a secretary, why?'

'He's already tried. For God's sake, Viv, cut me some slack. I'm helping, but there are . . .'

'Don't bother. I'll head up the hill. If that place is as big as you say it'll take time to check out the whole place. You do your stuff and get back to me when you can. I appreciate what you've done.'

He ran his hands through his hair and let go of a breath, 'Oh piss off. I have a conference call that involves half a dozen agencies and since it was me who set it up I thought it was only manners to speak to them myself to rearrange. I'm trying but . . . Oh, never mind. Let's get going.'

Her head thumped and her wrists were still sore, but at least the swelling on her leg had gone down. She was grateful that he was driving. She wasn't big on being driven, but she could just about cope with Mac at the wheel. As forecast, the sky looked heavy with the threat of snow. She shivered on the way to the car, and a nippy breeze caught her hair. The Audi's heater was almost as efficient as the Rav's and before they reached the turn-off in the village that would take them up to the Braes, the car was toasty warm.

'You think he'd kill her if he doesn't get what he wants?'

'I don't know. His motivation seems to be about the £500,000. But he could have weapons and if he's angry, well you know what he's capable of. That thump to your head wasn't exactly the act of a gentleman.'

'If he has weapons why didn't he use them on me? I didn't get any sense that he'd had special training. You know, like he had any strategy. He was just using brute force . . .'

'For God's sake, Viv, you don't have to feel bad about him overpowering you. It's happened to the best of us.'

'Yeah, sure. When were you last overpowered?'

He drummed on the steering wheel with his long elegant fingers. 'Eighteen months ago.'

She was shocked. He'd never said anything. But why would he if it was part of his job? Her work for him was unofficial she supposed, although she got paid handsomely for it. 'You never said.'

'There's a lot you don't know about me. As there's a lot about you I don't know. It's how this game works.'

'What game?'

He shook his head in frustration, then switched on his MP3. Mozart blasted from the speakers. Was he silencing her? The music was fine but she got tetchy in his immaculate car. It smelled of polish and something . . . lemony vinegary. When the hell did he get time to clean it? He certainly wasn't the type to have it valeted. There's no way he'd leave his precious wheels with strangers. Maybe the NTF had its own valet service, like Mand's ex's company. She assumed the NTF tracked their employees. But Mand's car, could it be bugged? She should keep her mind on the next move instead of going down the route of uber suspicion.

Mac parked and they walked alongside the gorse bushes to the first door of the bunker. It was padlocked. Mac patted his jacket pockets.

She said, 'No worries,' and rooted around in her bag before she found a set of picks.

He shook his head. 'You are utterly incorrigible.' He turned and stared up at the phone mast. 'You think this thing gives off harmful rays?'

She prodded around with the padlock and it clicked open. 'Yes. I absolutely do. We're being permeated by all sorts of rays all day every day, and some are harmful and others benign.' She glanced up at the mast, 'That thing. Just imagine what it is capable of. Can't be benign. Bouncing info off satellites thousands of miles away and vice versa. It'd be a no brainer to think that's safe. Come on, let's get away from the deadly rays.'

They slipped through the door into the dark, cold corridor. Viv used her phone to give them some light. When they reached the blast door it proved hard to shift, even with two of them. The local police must have tried to shut it tight but hadn't managed entirely.

Mac said, 'He probably planned your abduction in advance. There's no way he'd be able to lever this open without a crowbar. Although someone must have left it open wide enough for your woman to get inside. She didn't strike me as particularly tough.'

'Oh, I wouldn't bank on that. Sleeping rough is no life for sissies. And she carries . . .'

'What does she carry?'

'Nothing.'

'One of these days you're going to realise that I'm not the enemy. We're both singing from the same hymn-sheet.'

She snorted, 'You and your Hail Marys.'

He released a long, slow sigh. They reached the bunkroom and he switched the lights on. They flickered as if they were about to go out. 'You should try it some time. A few Hail Marys wouldn't do you any harm.' His voice echoed round the room. 'Can't imagine what it would be like here in a real emergency.'

She shot him a look.

'I meant being in here long term.'

'I see you've taken your sensitivity meds this morning.'

'I just mean . . . oh forget it.'

'Trust me I'm trying to, but the throbbing head, aching wrists and swollen leg are a minor distraction. Oh, and I wonder where I got those?'

He shook his head, 'I didn't mean . . . God, touchy or what? Let's take a look further along. See if we can get into any of the other rooms.'

The room where the woman had left stuff was as it had been. There was a chance that she'd return to retrieve things or maybe take up residence again. Although Viv imagined that once a sanctuary had had an intruder the woman would move on. They moved around checking as many rooms as they could get into. Easy to tell if a room had not been accessed recently since the dust build-up at the base of the door was undisturbed. After about half an hour of checking doors they realised that there was nothing more they could do.

As they hit daylight Viv's phone vibrated. 'Hi, Mand. Did you get it?'

'Yes.' She sounded stroppy. 'But it's not all I got.'

'Are you okay?'

'I'm fine, but she knew where she was sending us. The bureau is always locked, but only last week when we visited James was crawling about on the floor and pulled a key from beneath the bureau. She had stuck it there deliberately with Sellotape, but was furious when she found him sitting with it in his mouth. I don't think she was in the slightest bit worried about James. It was the key. Anyway, I knew where to look for it and with the account book was a bundle of letters tied up with red ribbon.'

'Have you got them?'

'Yes. It doesn't feel right, but yes I have and I'm on my way back. Have you heard . . .'

'Yes. He sent a video. You'll see it when you get here.'

'Right. Is there anything else I can do while I'm down here?'

Viv thought of how few clothes she'd packed but said, 'No. Just get yourselves back safe and sound.'

Mac said, 'Is she all right?'

'Yes. She's just a much better person than I am. I have no qualms about reading people's mail but she really does. She's bringing a bundle of letters.'

'Interesting. Meantime I'll try and locate a proper map of the bunkers nearest here. Best be methodical.' He made a call and then they returned to the cottage. Moll danced round Viv's legs and Viv, getting the message, put a lead on her and said, 'I'll take her round the River Park. Ten minutes tops.'

The ground was hard and rough, but it was great to be out and away from people. Didn't matter how much she liked someone she couldn't be cooped up with them without losing the will to live. Even a ten-minute walk could make her human again. She mulled over the conversation with Ruddy. There was no doubt now that her mum had worked in intelligence, she'd have to accept that, but what exactly had she done? Ruddy was younger than her mum so probably wouldn't have worked with her, but he knew of her. And what was that about 'them' having 'sorted it'; what exactly had they needed to sort? Why did the woman in the photograph give my mum lots of money? Nothing added up. If her attacker and his piano-playing brother were her sons, why hadn't she left her money to them? What had they done to deserve exclusion from their inheritance? Maybe Germans had a different attitude to inheritance. She mustn't assume that every country had the same bizarre system as the UK.

Moll ran ahead, her muzzle shifting from side to side, drawing in whatever smells were there. Once Viv reached the Teith she sat on a log that had been hewn into a rough bench for fishermen. She drank in the cold crisp air. This kind of day, with a clear blue sky, was a precious thing in a Scottish winter. Dark peaty water raced by and ducks landed against the flow before drifting back downstream without a care in the world. Moll became restless and pulled at her lead. They continued along the riverbank, Viv trying to rid herself of the frustration born of impotence. She was a woman of action and while thinking was a good thing, she couldn't stand this business of going over and over the same things and reaching the same conclusion unless it led to action.

Her mum had obviously worked for British Intelligence. She'd been on 'missions' abroad and at home, and on one or more of these missions she'd encountered the woman in the photograph. For some reason the woman had left Viv's mum a wodge of cash, which her son, Viv's attacker, believed belonged to him. Now what about the brother? Did he believe the same? Was he asking questions about Viv so that he and his brother could get closer to their inheritance? Maybe one brother didn't know what the other was doing. She remembered the newspaper article about the skirmish at a concert hall in Berlin. Hadn't that been the pianist with his brother? Worth checking. Her phone vibrated. It was Mac wondering where she was.

'Sorry, I'll turn back.' She tugged on Moll's lead and pulled her to take a different route home. She'd been longer than she'd planned, but felt better for untangling some of the mash in her head. She slipped off her coat inside the porch. Mac had his phone pinned to his ear as a car arrived. She opened the door to Mand with James and his endless bags of kit.

Mand dumped most of the stuff on the floor in the hallway, but gestured with her head for Viv to follow. They went into the kitchen and Mand sat James on the floor then pulled out a bundle of letters from her handbag, their yellowing paper bound by a red ribbon; an indication that they were not recent.

'You can read these if you want. I don't think it's right. They're probably private from dad to mum. And this is the account book.'

Viv glanced at the top envelope. It had an internal services postmark. Mand was probably right. It would be a breach of privacy to go through them. 'Let's have coffee and food. We can decide what to do with the account book. I'll let you see the video he sent.'

Viv pulled out her phone and played the thirty seconds of video. Mand started to cry. Viv rubbed her back. 'He hasn't hurt her and he has tied her hands in front of her, which means she's not in serious discomfort.'

'How can you say that? She's being held by some nut job, God knows where. She'll be freezing. You know she dresses for the tropics because of the Pound. Thin trousers and a tee shirt in these temperatures.'

'She has a coat on.'

Mand spun round. 'You think that's enough? It's minus four out there today. She'll die of hypothermia.'

'Someone was here earlier. He said we shouldn't underestimate her. She's been well trained.'

'She might well have been but that was years ago. Now she's an old woman.'

'I wouldn't let her hear you say that. She'd have your guts for garters.'

Mand snorted, 'I haven't heard that saying for a long time. Didn't grannie used to say that?'

Viv nodded, 'She did, and she meant it. Now let's get some coffee. You did a good job finding the account book. As for these,' she patted the pile of letters, 'we'll make a decision later.'

Mac joined them, 'Ruddy . . . shit, I must stop calling him that. The boss said that she's used a couple of code words.'

Viv spun round. 'Really?'

'Yep, if an agent uses "please" it means that they believe they're safe. So if she thinks she's safe he probably doesn't have a weapon, like a gun that could discharge by accident or a knife . . . We'll have to trust her, Viv.'

A loaded silence expanded between them. Then she said, 'What else did she say. I mean what was that "one swallow" stuff?'

'In old speak a swallow was a female operative sent into the field to seduce information out of someone.'

'There's no way my mum would do that. No way.' She shook her head trying to rid herself of an uncomfortable image. 'Shit. This is horrible.'

Mac said, 'Look, seduction takes different forms. It's not necessarily sexual. She could entice information out of him without . . .'

'No, don't even say that out loud. It's my mum we're talking about.' She rubbed her face viciously then squealed as she caught the sore side of her head. 'What else did Ruddy say?'

He hesitated, 'Nothing really; that was it.'

'Why do I get the feeling that that's not quite true?'

'Because you're a mistress of suspicion.'

She chewed on her lip and went back to making coffee.

Mac flicked through the bundle of letters. 'I don't think they can be from your dad.'

'Why not?'

'Because they've all come from the same place and your dad worked all over. If they were from him the postmarks would differ.'

'But I thought the service had internal postmarks.'

'They do, but there's a number to indicate which station they've come through. These are all from the same one.'

Mand said, 'I don't know what any of that means.'

Viv said, 'She knew that whoever went for the account book would find these letters. She knows that we'll have them. Maybe sending us for the book was a sign. Maybe there's something in the letters that will help us to find her.'

Mand said, 'You're just determined to read them. They are private. Even if they're not from dad.'

'But if they're not from dad then . . .'

'Then what? She was having an affair with someone?'

'I don't know, but if we read at least one it will give us some idea.'

Mand stomped off into the conservatory with James on her hip. Mac had lit the wood-burning stove earlier and between that and the Aga the place was toasty warm. The look on Mac's face was one she'd seen before. He was holding something back from her but his face gave him away. No poker for Mac.

'What? What is going on with you?'

'I've already said, if this wasn't about your mum you'd handle it differently.'

'Of course I would. Wouldn't anyone? She's my mother. This isn't some stranger that I have no emotional tie to.'

Her phone buzzed. She took off to answer it.

'Viv? I have a message from Kurt Hahn,' Jinty said, at the other end of a poor connection.

Viv put a finger up to her ear to block out Mand's chatter with James. 'Jinty? What does he want?'

'He told me to say that you shouldn't do anything and definitely not give him any money.' Jinty sounded confused.

'Can I contact Mr Hahn?'

'Yes. But he's rehearsing, then playing today and tomorrow, so his phone will be off most of the time. You can send him an email. I'm forwarding his address to you right now. I didn't want to give out any of your details. It's all very cryptic. Are you okay?'

'It's a long story and I'm sorry that you've been drawn into it.'

'No probs, Viv, as long as you're okay . . . You know Andrew would help if you needed him to.'

'That's really kind, but I think we'll be fine.' She didn't sound convincing. 'Although, if things aren't fine I might take you up on that offer.'

Her email pinged with the arrival of Jinty's message. 'Thanks. That email has arrived. I'll fill you in on your next hair date.'

'Looking forward.'

Viv turned back into the kitchen. 'New development. Nut job's brother wants to give us advice.'

Mac screwed up his forehead. 'The pianist brother?'

She nodded. 'Yes, he said we've not to give him any money. I'll try and speak to him just now.'

She got hold of her laptop and sent a message from an account that she kept specifically for this kind of use. She didn't imagine becoming chums with Mr Hahn any time soon.

'Sounded as if he's warning you about his brother. I mean if they were in this together he wouldn't have said that.'

'Jinty said that he's rehearsing and playing concerts over the next couple of days, which would also make me think he's not involved, but that could just be his cover story. Convenient to say you'd be wrapped up. He could be anywhere. We don't have to trust him. He hasn't given us grounds to.'

'Has he given you grounds not to, though?'

'Only that he was data harvesting.' She mimed quote marks.

Mac laughed. 'You mean asking for your number?'

'No, I mean he was grilling Jinty about me. She was worried so didn't tell him anything. But he already knew where I lived, otherwise he wouldn't have paid me a visit.'

'Are you absolutely sure it was him?'

'I don't know too many tall blond Germanic-looking men, but no I'm not absolutely sure.'

'Okay, so what have we got on him apart from him asking questions about you?'

'He's a concert pianist, plays plink plonky sort of stuff so has limited appeal, but seems to get bookings if what Jinty said is true. He was off to London to continue his tour. We can easily find out about that.'

She Googled his name and up came a list of dates for concerts in the south and south west. 'Looks as if he is on tour, but let's not be too hasty in making him a good guy.'

'What did you ask him in the email?'

'What he wants. Why is he giving us advice instead of stopping his brother from . . . whatever?'

'You think he can control his brother any more than you can control Mand?' He nodded in the direction of the conservatory.

'No, I suppose not, but I want . . . ' She rubbed her face, wincing as she caught the bruise on the side of her head. 'Oh God, I just want my mum to be okay.'

He stepped closer to her and laid his hand on her back, 'Well, I've got some real map references, so why don't we take action on those and leave the pianist 'til later?'

'I thought you were busy with stuff?'

'I am busy with stuff,' he drew out the word in the same sarcastic way she had. 'But that stuff doesn't matter to me as much as this stuff does, so are we going or aren't we?'

She nodded and slipped her jacket back on. 'Mand, could you feed Moll at five if we're not back? We should be, but just in case.'

Mand snapped back, 'Are you sure you trust me to?'

Moll trotted out from her bed and nuzzled Viv's hand. Viv sighed and bent down to rub the dog's ears. 'Come on, Mand, this is difficult for everyone. Make sure you all stay safe and locked up.'

'Why? D'you think he'll come here again?'

'I've no idea what he'll do. He's a loose cannon and we don't want to make this whole debacle easier for him. Sal has a collection of DVDs in that cupboard. Check them out. You and James could watch *The Sound of Music* or something.'

'Don't worry about us, we'll keep ourselves occupied.'

Viv and Mac headed to his car, but before they got in Viv ran back for her laptop. She returned, jumped in and pulled the seatbelt over her shoulder. 'Actually I'd like to do a bit more digging about this brother. We don't even know his name. I need a Wifi hotspot. Sal's keeps giving up.'

'Okay, I've got something to check out anyway.'

'And what would that be?'

'There's a joint churches' meeting in the hall next to the post office. Someone just might have noticed your mum with her secret friend at the service. You know what small communities are like. Everyone knows everyone and everything.'

She screwed up her eyes at him. She wasn't convinced, but said, 'Okay.

Drop me at the café on the main street. I'd like at least an hour.'

'Fine.'

The café was busy, but there was a small table by a radiator so she plonked herself down. A waitress handed her a menu.

'Actually, I'd just like a flat white, if you do them?'

'Sure. I'll get that for you.'

The Wifi code was on the specials' blackboard. She logged on and began to dig. Her first port of call was Kurt Hahn's Facebook page. Both his profile and his professional page were up to date, which was good since it meant he was a regular participant or someone was on his behalf. The downside was she had a ton of irrelevant stuff to scroll through before she eventually found what she was looking for – press coverage of the fight he'd had in the foyer of the concert hall in Berlin. It speculated that the other man had been Kurt's brother. She should have followed up on this earlier. She cursed herself for being off form. Not any more though. Her hackles were up and she was determined to know all there was to know about the Hahns. By sheer luck, when she Googled Kurt Hahn another Hahn, first name Kristian, came up, also with a Facebook page. His privacy settings were more difficult to infiltrate. She could see immediately why the brothers might fight. Kurt showed all the signs of being a liberal European, Kristian . . . not so much. His interests were so far to the right he was off the page. Why the hell hadn't she done this sooner?

She scrolled through endless posts that confirmed Kristian's political leanings as anti-European. There were a few photographs of him with other men. Neither brother had posted anything to do with relationships and there were no photographs of women on Kristian's pages. The females on Kurt's pages were of him with fans or sponsors. She'd psyched herself up for swastikas, but there were none. The AfD were a new far right party who claimed to be on the side of Germany's youth. Kristian was a supporter, but hadn't been posting politically active stuff for a couple of years. Every political post was dated to 2015. He'd obviously been on a roll then, but it had subsided or gone underground. The latter would be more worrying.

She found an email address, illegally; needs must. She hacked in and was searching before her flat white arrived. 'Thanks.'

'Can I get you anything else?'

'No thanks, I'm fine for now.'

It was amazing what you could tell about someone's life by tying their conversations to their buying history. Kristian wasn't a big spender on luxury goods, but he was fond of online gambling. That could do a lot of damage to a man's already depleted bank account. She discovered an email spat between the brothers that took place just before the fight in the foyer. It always seemed to be about money. Kristian accusing Kurt of having loads of money and not helping him out of a fix. Kurt denying that he had such funds and why should he rescue him again. A familiar family story. There was no sign that Kristian had been in the military or the police, but he certainly believed in his own right to superiority. A more recent spat showed the brothers having yet another conversation about money. She sat back and sipped her coffee. Kurt was obviously fed up trying to placate his brother. Every angle Kurt took to reason with him was met with an immature, 'you always say that' or 'you never do this'. Kristian didn't take responsibility for anything; he liked to blame. She scrolled through the email history in search of a clue as to what was happening five or more years ago, but the account didn't go back that far. However, she did find an early email to someone who had copied in another email address, which Kristian reminded him was out of use – no such thing as deleted. She began another search. This bit of her work was time-consuming but nine times out of ten fruitful. Bingo, she struck gold.

Their mother died. Still no love lost, but the beginning of another fight about money. Kurt assuring Kristian that it would all come right in the end. Kristian not believing a word of it and right in his assertions, as it turned out. Neither son was mentioned in her will, at least not as a beneficiary. That must have been painful. From Kurt's tone it was as if he hadn't expected anything. Maybe he'd had a conversation with her when she'd made her intentions clear. Speculation, speculation, speculation. The bottom line was, they each got zilch but Kristian was the only one to appear shocked. So either Kurt already knew the contents of the will or didn't care. There could be many reasons for not caring, so it wasn't safe to assume he had enough money of his own not to have to worry. Kristian had set his sights on a windfall and was up to his eyes in debts that he couldn't clear. A picture was building of Kristian as a man in serious trouble. Had he gone to a loan shark? Was his life in danger? It would seem from his aggression that he was desperate. That £500,000 would go a long way to alleviate most troubles.

The door to the café swung open and Mac strode in and sank into the seat opposite her. 'You done?'

She said, 'You need coffee?'

He shrugged, 'Yes. You want another?'

The waitress arrived with a menu but he shook his head. 'Just coffees. Same again?'

Viv nodded.

He said, 'Another two of those thanks.'

The waitress walked off and he said, 'How are you getting on? Find anything?'

'Just confirmation of Kristian's dire financial state. Got a problem with the gee- gees.'

Mac laughed, 'I've not heard that for a while. Real gee-gees or online?'

'Both. He has a few direct debits to online gambling sites and a couple of turf accounts. Once a gambler you lose your sense of discretion. I think he'd bet on a spider race if he got the chance.'

'Well, d'you want to hear what I've got?'

She tutted, 'See you and your withholding, Freud would have a field day. So who was he?'

'He's got a cottage on the north side of the village. Name's Cochrane, Colonel Cochrane.'

Viv raised her eyebrows, 'Shall we go and see him?'

'Why not? But let's get coffee down us first.'

The waitress arrived with two steaming cups and placed them on the table.

'Actually, I'll have a slice of that ginger tray-bake, thanks.' He gestured to Viv.

'No, I'm fine. I'll just have a wee sliver of yours.'

He shook his head. 'I thought you might.'

The sky was overcast, heavy with rain or more likely snow, since the temperature was still below freezing. They drove out of the village, following directions that Mac had gleaned from one of the congregation. A long bumpy track wound its way up into the hills. Hailstones began to bounce off the windscreen and within seconds the track ahead was white. Mac sat forward, but the wipers made very little difference to the visibility. He slowed to a crawl, but the hail became thicker, each piece the size of a small gobstopper. The noise of it battering against the roof drowned out all possibility of continuing a conversation. A few smaller tracks led off to wooden sheds and buildings. One looked like a rundown stable or hay store, but it was difficult to tell. Eventually they reached a fork and Mac crawled along the right-hand lane. They continued on an even bumpier track, with a camber so steep the car began to lean at a forty-five-degree angle. Mac just avoided ending in the ditch and no more. The hail turned to snowflakes.

Mac resumed the conversation. 'Might be better to turn back. I've no idea what terrain we're in for up ahead.'

Viv scanned the sky, still heavy in every direction as far as the eye could see. 'We'll have to go on to find somewhere to turn. There's no way we can do it along this stretch. How does anyone do this drive every day? It's got to knacker the undercarriage of any car.'

Mac pointed. 'That helps.' An old long-based Land Rover sitting alongside a stone farmhouse came into view. The house was too big to be called a cottage, but it wasn't grand. A bank of trees, rapidly turning white, shielded it from the west wind and a lawn of sorts ran round the whole place. The front door opened as they parked.

'I wondered how long it would take you to show up. Come on in.' The man's Scottish public-school accent was clipped and clear. 'Here, take a seat through in the kitchen where it's warm.'

They made their way to a spacious but gloomy room, where a collie and a lab stirred from a large raised bed at the end of an ancient Aga. An Aga was obviously a prerequisite for living in the wilds. She knew people in the city who had them as fashion accessories, like a Louis Vuitton bag. Completely unnecessary in houses with cavity-wall insulation and central heating, but here it was probably the only source of heat. That their host was wearing a rough tweed jacket, a jumper and a flannel shirt with a cravat was telling. Also the dogs had no sooner had a sniff than they retreated to their bed adjacent to the warming oven. The man urged her to take a seat, which she did reluctantly, since the Aga seemed to have little impact on most of the room.

He brushed his hand over a scar on the side of his face. 'Tea?'

Mac said, 'No, no thanks, we've just had coffee.'

Cochrane said, 'Well, I'm guessing he came for her then?'

Mac said, 'Yes. So she knew he would?'

He nodded. 'Has she told you anything?'

Viv shook her head. 'No, but we've had a video from him demanding money.'

'She said he'd be after the cash. Can't blame him really. I mean he had no idea why his mother would cut him out of her will. And to find out it went to a complete stranger. Well, she wasn't a stranger to your mum, but in his eyes she was. She knew there'd be trouble; thought it would come sooner than this.'

Viv said, 'I think he's desperate now. Maybe before he was able to tick along, but not now.'

'Do you know this for sure?'

Viv nodded.

'She's been digging,' Mac said. 'Nothing is sacred if Viv's on the case.'

'Like mother like daughter then.'

'I wish people wouldn't compare me to her.'

'You should be proud to have a mother like her.'

His defensive tone was unexpected. Who the hell did he think he was to make judgements about her and her mother? Had he been more than an old friend to her mum? Lives were complicated sequences of events; nothing went in a straight line unless you were dead. She was doubtful of so many things about her mum, her work, her relationships, but most of all how her dad had fitted into it all. On the surface their marriage had looked solid. Was there reason to doubt that?

'Greta. That was her name. I mean probably not her real name but her cover. She and your mum . . .'

Viv urged, 'What? They what?'

His eyes bored into hers. 'They respected each other. They both knew they had a job to do. They both believed in fighting for their own countries. They knew that whatever they'd been sent to do was in the interest of their own national security.'

Viv groaned, 'Oh God, not that old rubbish.'

He didn't flinch or raise his voice. 'I get the feeling you don't feel the same way about your country.'

Viv shot back, 'Don't you judge me. I'm willing to go a long way for this country, but only with specifics. Not interested in huge generalisations like our "national security". I want to know exactly what she was doing. I want to know exactly what I'm getting into when . . . shit! We don't have to talk about me; we have to find her.'

Mac said, 'So she was expecting one of the sons to turn up at some point? Did they contest the will?'

'It was messy at the time, but it was dealt with. Your mother didn't want the money. She made sure the community got it.'

'Now you've lost me. She handed the whole lot over to a community? Where? Berlin? Some small town in Germany?'

He shook his head. 'No, a small town not a million miles from here.'

Viv stood with her mouth open. Mac put his finger under her chin. 'You look like a guppy.'

She brushed him away and said, 'Surely not Doune?'

'No, not Doune.'

She blew out a breath. 'So where? You obviously know about it.'

He flashed a look at Mac, 'The money's been invested. It's no longer anything to do with Trude.'

Viv bristled at the sound of her mum's name. No one called her Trude but her dad. She thought about the letters and the account book, which clearly had nothing in it. 'What can you tell us that might help us to find her?'

As if he'd made a decision that Viv was on the right side of the angels he rolled his shoulders and said, 'Greta was kept in protective custody near Comrie. If she told her sons about that well . . . maybe . . .'

Mac said, 'Thanks, we'll get a look at Cultybraggan.' He gestured for Viv to leave.

Once in the car she yelled, 'For fuck sake, anyone would think we were the enemy! You'd think they'd just want her to be safe, but no they just want to cover their backs.'

Daylight was fading as they edged their way out of the house's drive onto the track, now a couple of inches deep in snow which was still pouring down.

Mac was sombre. 'You're not being fair. They signed the OSA and took that very seriously. Even when someone's life is in danger they won't give anything away, regardless of who's asking. Old school.'

'That's bullshit and you know it. I have clearance. I know how this works and if one of your own is in danger . . . Oh, never mind, why am I telling you what you already know? Stop feeding me BS and let's go over to this . . . Culty . . .'

'Cultybraggan. It's a huge camp about fifteen miles from here.'

'And you didn't think to mention this before?'

'I did think of it, but it's occupied, so I thought it unlikely. In fact it's been bought by . . .' he hesitated, 'the community.'

'Christ, Mac, what the . . . Let's take a look.'

Mac switched his radio on and caught the end of a weather forecast: 'Snow drifting on minor roads will not be cleared by ploughs until much later tonight.' He glanced at Viv. 'We have to drive across a high route to get to the camp. It's not wise. This thing doesn't have snow tyres on it yet.'

Viv shook her head. 'The Rav has all-weather tyres. Let's go back and get it.'

It was impossible to see where the ditch started and the road ended. Snow swirled and blew, looking beautiful, but a real nuisance when you were trying to get anywhere. Gradually, inch by inch, they crawled their way back to the main road in the village, which hadn't seen a plough yet. This was definitely the kind of powdery alpine snow that would compact, and if it froze there'd be trouble getting up and down the lane to Sal's cottage. He stopped the car at the entrance to the estate. 'We can leave this here. If I take it any further and we get stuck we might not get yours out.'

They both jumped out, huddled their collars up to their chins and walked the rest of the way. Molly barked as they approached and Mand came to the window.

She swung the door open. 'Wow, this is a real change. James is captivated. It's the first time he's seen snow. I didn't bring a snowsuit for him to go out in.'

Viv said, 'We never had snowsuits. We had woollen gloves and only came home when we were totally soaking and had chilblains.'

Mand said, 'That was then; this is now.'

Viv said, 'I'd feel better if you stayed indoors anyway. Mac and I are going to check out another place, a camp, if we can get to it.'

'Don't you go taking unnecessary risks. It's bad enough having mum in danger.'

Mac nipped to the loo so as to avoid the crossfire. When he returned Viv was standing by the door with her car key in her hand and her rucksack over her shoulder.

She patted the side of the sack. 'Everything we could ever need is inside this.' She threw the key to Mac. 'Best if you drive.'

He caught the key and said, 'Honoured indeed.'

'Lock everything up when we leave. It's not worth taking any chances.'

Chapter Fourteen

The Rav had traction so they would be safe to drive in most conditions.

'We should go the long way round, via Crieff. I don't fancy our chances over the moor. There's a sheer drop on the south side that not even the Rav could cope with.'

Viv said, 'Okay, if you say so. You know the area better than me. I'd rather we got there in one piece.'

The motorway had been gritted but was already down to one lane. The snow was blowing from the east and building up really quickly. They didn't have to be on the motorway for long and within five minutes Mac pointed to a sign. 'We go off here.'

The slip road was even more dodgy, but he slowed and continued through the village of Greenloaning. Nothing green about it today. The windscreen wipers were going nineteen to the dozen and he was only just managing to see the road.

'God, the snow takes over so quickly. No road markings; no sign of the pavement. The only good thing about it is movement of anything will leave prints.'

Mac was sombre. 'We can't be sure she's at Cultybraggan. There are a few other derelict camps on the Carse. He could have taken her to any of them. Culty is the only one that's still being used. I'd be surprised if he took her there. People would notice his movements and ask questions.'

'He could easily make up a story, an excuse for being there. Research usually covers it.'

Mac nodded. 'He doesn't strike me as the type to get involved with explanations. He'd planned your attack, but the bunker on the route for the run was probably a lucky coincidence.'

The snow continued to pelt against the windscreen. He was down to twenty miles an hour. 'This is tricky. I didn't see a forecast for a whiteout, did you?'

He shook his head, '"The possibility of a few flurries" of snow was how they put it. Although they always say something different for the "high ground", whatever that means. This,' he gestured ahead, 'doesn't strike me as particularly high, but what do I know? You're the mountaineer.'

'Bull. Why do people confuse climbers with mountaineers? They're not the same breed. As a climber I'd rather be airlifted into the bottom of a climb and airlifted back out from the top. A mountaineer would enjoy all the struggle of getting there over rough terrain, doing the walk or climb, abbing off and walking back out. Not for me, matey.'

The snow was driving across the fields and building up against the fence. They had to slow to a crawl, since it obscured where the road ended and the verge began. Viv sat forward with her eyes next to the glass, but it made no difference. Mac dipped the headlights which helped, but there was no let-up. It was beautiful.

'D'you want to stop or turn around? This is precarious.'

'I'll keep on for a few minutes. We're not far from Crieff now. Glad I brought this' He tapped the screen of the sat nav.

'Good luck trusting one of those.'

Within minutes Crieff came into view and as soon as they were sheltered on each side by buildings, the road edges became visible and the going easier. It was like travelling through a ghost town, the good people of Perthshire heeding the latest local warnings to stay off the roads. Even if she'd heard warnings Viv couldn't have remained at home waiting. She was like a cat on hot bricks, her head flicking from side to side, checking for signs of a black pick-up truck. He could be anywhere; the last sighting was so long ago and God knows how many black pick-ups were out there. Mac had the blower on full blast to stop the inside of the windows from steaming up but it was still difficult to see clearly with snow pelting down. Wherever the German had her mum she hoped there was some form of heating. Mac's phone rang and he switched it on to speaker.

Ruddy's voice made her pay attention.

'We've got some info back on the video. The sound guys say that it was made underground. They can tell from the amount of echo or the absence thereof that it was made where there are soft furnishings. Probably a carpet on the floor and maybe wall hangings. Your best bet in the area is Cultybraggan. Keep me posted.' He hung up.

'That's good news. I thought it was a shot in the dark.'

'I was just thinking about how cold she'll be. Carpets would make a small difference.'

'If there are carpets it's because someone has invested in it. That could also mean heating that works and loos. Remember he needs amenities as well.'

They reached a road sign almost covered by snow but with the 'Com' still discernible.

Mac said, 'About eight miles to go. Not easy miles, but we should be fine.'

Viv, aware of doubt in his voice, 'This is the safest way, isn't it?'

'Yes. Like I said, the road over the moor would've been madness. If it gets too bad she'll let us know.' He pointed again to the sat nav.

Viv shook her head. 'I'm amazed that you'd rely on that at all.'

Mac grinned. 'Don't knock it. She's got me out of a few fixes.'

'I'd have thought your sense of direction was pretty good.'

'Why thank you; compliment accepted.'

She tutted, 'You can't be in your position and not have a great sense of direction. It was one of my tests.'

'What tests?'

She slid round in her seat and stared at him, 'You know fine well what tests.'

'I don't. I've no idea what you're on about unless you've been through the . . . was it at Tulliallan?'

'No, although I have been to Tully.'

'So you've been on the "special" training course?'

'Maybe you're not supposed to know what training I've had.'

He sighed, 'All I need to know is that Ruddy, as you so fondly call him, seems to trust you and in this game that's 99 per cent of the trick.'

She snorted, 'You think? I get the trust thing but . . .'

'No, there are no buts. If he didn't trust you it wouldn't matter how good you were at the old hacking and info gathering, he couldn't afford to have you on board. Now this thing with your mum . . .'

'What? What thing with my mum? What difference does that make?'

'Well, he already let you know that he knew your dad, and now you know that he also knows your mum.'

'God, you make it sound like nepotism. Like I only get work cos they know my folks. I totally hate that.'

He shook his head, 'Christ, Viv, no matter how well he knew your family, if you were not the right person for the job he wouldn't entertain you, so shut up with the nepotism crap. You're working on your own merit, end of.'

She chewed the inside of her cheek. 'I'm pretty freaked out to think about her as a spy. Maybe there's been some mistake and she really was a secretary.'

Mac laughed, 'You're brilliant at making up stories to fit your needs.'

'Then I'm no different from anyone else.'

'Except you are totally different from most people and that's why you get to go on "special" training and whatever else he's had you do without me knowing about it. It's only in this one case, because it's your mum, that you can't separate your emotional attachment . . .'

She interrupted him, 'I don't ever see any benefit in trying to separate emotion from reason. It's not possible. All you do is privilege one over the other, but neither goes away and in my world it's always better to remain aware of both equally. D'you remember at uni when that professor of philosophy went ape shit because he thought he was being accused of not being objective?'

He said, 'Yeah, I think I do remember something about that.'

'Well, he only went ape shit because he valued, and I mean overvalued, reason and undervalued emotion. He was determined to be a man of the "Enlightenment". He just didn't get that things had moved on. God, he was nuts. Still saw women as overly emotional. I think he was "retired", thank God. Total dinosaur.'

'Well now that's him sorted, we should be approaching Cultybraggan.' He glanced at the sat nav screen and pointed again. 'It's in here somewhere.'

The rooftops of Comrie were just visible on the right. Mac drove away from the town and on across a flat plain, the snow driving from the east. As they began to climb into an area of trees with a sharp bend off to the right Mac spotted an MOD sign.

He pointed, 'There. That's where we're going. Trust the sat nav now?'

She didn't answer, but stared at rows and rows of strange rounded huts covered in snow that made the place look like a scene from Disney. They reached the narrow entrance where a sentry box stood forlorn and a rusted barrier was up, so they drove straight ahead.

Viv pointed to the road. 'One set of fresh tyre tracks either going in or coming out.'

Mac followed the tracks rapidly being eliminated by a fresh layer of snow. They reached a large building like an aircraft hangar with sliding doors. A tiny gap in the side let light out. Someone was here. Two fabulous shepherd's huts, their wheelbases packed with snow, were parked to the side. The smaller of the two had steps at one end. Viv thought it would make an amazing travelling office. The other hut, twice the size, had steps up at the side and smoke coming from a small metal chimney on the roof. Mac stopped the Rav and they fastened up to their chins and jumped out. Heads down they ran towards the gap in the hangar doors from where the sound of some sort of music drifted out. The pair could see another couple of shepherds' huts in the process of construction, and not yet on wheelbases. They stamped their feet to knock the snow off and to get the attention of anyone there.

A woman wearing dungarees, a thick jumper, heavy soled boots and a hat with flaps that covered her ears came from behind one of the huts holding a plane for working the wood.

'Hi. What can I do for you?' She tucked a stray hair into her hat with a grubby hand encased in a fingerless glove.

Mac said, 'We're looking for a man with a black pick-up.'

She nodded. 'I don't know who was driving it, but there has been one here.'

Viv said, 'Has been? Does that mean he's gone?'

'I couldn't say. I only saw the truck once and it was late into the night.'

'Where was that exactly?'

'It drove towards the bunker. Assumed it must be the new owner or something.'

Mac said, 'Where is the bunker?'

The woman walked to the door and pointed. 'See that fence? There's an entrance about a hundred metres along. It's chained with a padlock.'

Viv said, 'Thank you, that's great.'

They got back into the Rav and drove towards a twelve-foot high fence with a roll of razor wire at the top. Not clear whether they were on tarmac or not Mac edged the Rav along the fence until they reached the entrance. No tracks here. Not a good sign. The door sat within a discreet alcove. There was no evidence of a chain, so Viv scraped back some snow on the ground and uncovered it lying near the entrance. She examined the links. Bolt cutters had been used to sever them, so not the owner with a key who'd been in the middle of the night. Mac pulled at the door but it wouldn't budge. Viv got behind him and gave it her best shot as well. Nothing doing, but there were marks on the ground so it had been moved recently. Like the blast door on the other bunker this one weighed a ton and there was no way they would shift it without a crowbar.

Viv said, 'Let's ask her if she has anything we could borrow.'

They jumped back into the Rav and spun back round to the hangar.

The woman came to meet them. 'Any luck?'

'Not yet. You don't have a crowbar handy?'

She creased her eyebrows.

Mac said, 'We're with the police.' He produced his ID.

She hesitated, but gave a curt nod. 'I'll get it.' She strode over to the far side of the hangar where all manner of tools were hanging on hooks. She brought back a long metal bar with a thin edge at one end. 'This do?'

'Perfect,' Viv said. 'We'll bring it back when we're done.'

This time they managed to lever the door and scrape it towards them far enough to squeeze inside. In its early days the now-damaged seal on the inside would have prevented them doing this. They walked down a long corridor with the torch on Viv's phone lighting the way, until they reached the next blast door.

'God, they weren't taking any chances with the doors, were they.'

'That was the point. Those privileged enough to get inside were safe and nothing was supposed to get to them.'

Viv was scornful. 'You think it would have worked? I mean in the event of an actual nuke how long would it take for the earth out there,' she pointed to where they entered 'to be safe enough to live off again?' She blew out a long breath, the idea incomprehensible to her. 'Madness. Total madness.'

Mac said, 'I bet he's a man of routine. Worth going straight to the bunkroom where he kept you.'

Unlike the Doune bunker there was no light switch for the corridor but the floors were carpeted and the walls looked as if they'd been newly painted white. Mac led the way past doors on either side with signs indicating what each was used for. Laundry, Boiler room, Water processing, Studio, and eventually they came to a room marked 'Male bunks'. He pulled the door open and stepped inside, immediately putting out his arm to stop Viv coming any further. 'Wait.'

Viv muscled round him and caught her breath. He grabbed her arm but she pulled free, whimpering, 'No.'

On one of the bunks in the farthest corner someone lay on their back, a blanket covering them completely. Viv rushed forward and lifted the blanket to reveal the head. 'Bastard! What a bastard!' She yelled as she yanked the blanket clear of a blow-up doll. 'He's playing games now.'

Mac rubbed his long fingers over her back. 'Let's check for any minute thing that he's left behind.' He took out his own phone and used the torch to search the floor. It was a large carpeted room with sixteen bunks, each with a small locker by its side. The temperature was above what it was out of doors, but not comfortable in the least.

Viv crawled over the floor on her hands and knees and eventually held up a sliver of red polythene between her fingernails. 'Think he's been eating a Kit-Kat. We'll have to hope that he's the caring sharing type.'

Mac handed her an evidence bag. 'You never know what we'll need in the end. Stick it in there. It could have a partial on it.'

Mr Hahn was tidy and nothing else came up in the rest of the room. They made their way to a door marked 'Showers'. One of the cubicles was still damp and Viv checked the plug for hair and discovered some too pale to be his.

'This is encouraging. Could be mum's.'

Mac handed her another evidence bag. She carefully placed the hair inside and handed both bags back. He tucked them into an inside pocket and wandered off.

Viv said, 'Where are you going? It's clear they're not here.'

'Just let's take a look and see if they've used a kitchen. They have to eat and it's more anonymous to shop in a supermarket than to buy a takeaway. He can't be that careful.'

They discovered a room that reminded Viv of the dinner hall at primary school. A huge room with long Formica tables and benches either side. A large hatch at one end of the room opened onto an industrial sized kitchen with wall to wall stainless steel work tops, sinks, ovens and hobs. Nothing looked as if it had been touched since it was built. There was evidence of inactivity. Even though the building was supposed to be hermetically sealed dust had gathered along the entrances to rooms which told them that no one had crossed the threshold for a long time. Another huge room had boxes of equipment piled high. Everything completely out of date. Analogue tape decks, fax machines, computer screens all now museum pieces. A smaller radio room set up with recording gear, even microphones in situ, felt like a weird snapshot in time.

'Come on, let's get going. She's not here. He has her somewhere and the longer we waste here the further away he could get. We need to find them. Did you bring a map with the other military facilities with you?'

Mac tapped the screen of his phone. 'Got them downloaded on here. No signal in here, though. Let's go.'

Snow had already built up against the outside door and it took both of their strength to push it open. Mac managed to lever it shut with the crowbar before they drove back to the hangar to return it. No sign of the woman, so they propped it up against the wall where she'd kept it. Mac found the map on his phone and pointed to two places that were options for Hahn. He drove back out of the camp toward Crieff at a snail's pace. Driving snow was banked higher up against the fence forcing the road down to one lane and even that side was filling up fast.

Viv said, 'Do you think we could call in some favours?'

Mac turned to look at her. 'Who owes you?'

She swore silently. 'Oh, I don't know, but surely we can get help.'

He didn't answer and sat as far forward in his seat as he could.

She said, 'This is mad, isn't it. We need a helicopter with heat detection.'

Mac snorted, 'You're kidding me. Nothing is getting off the ground in this weather.'

She bit the inside of her cheek. He was right of course, but she didn't want to hear it. There had to be a way of finding them. It should be child's play. By the time they reached Crieff the whole place was a winter wonderland. No longer evidence of pavements, Hansel and Gretel cottages, and cars sitting in drives with at least a foot of snow on top. Every shop and pub was closed. Lights in every house made them look inviting. Viv felt like a voyeur, peering in through open curtains, watching families staring at screens. A weird silence, dense and impenetrable, had descended with the thick snow and it seemed as if everyone had battened down the hatches, prepared to wait it out. At the other side of Crieff a snowplough passed and Mac decided that the best thing to do was follow it towards the motorway. Their only hope of getting anywhere was on the motorway and even then they'd be lucky if it was being cleared regularly enough to be anything more than one lane.

'We're at the mercy of the weather, Viv. I know you don't want to hear this, but I think we should head home until this goes off. The worst case scenario would be us getting stuck up some country lane.' He grinned. 'Or maybe not so bad . . .'

She play-punched his arm. 'In your dreams. I hate to admit it, but you're probably right. Christ, it's impossible to see anything on either side of us. If we weren't behind him,' she pointed to the snowplough, 'we'd be up the creek. Okay, let's head back. See if we can find anything that would help work out his next move.' She rubbed her face and flinched again as she caught the bruise on the side of her head. 'This shouldn't be this difficult.'

'Sometimes it just is what it is.'

'Oh, wise words, master.'

'Sarcasm'll get you everywhere.'

She glanced at him and reminded herself how good it was to have him around. Her leg ached, as did her head. It would be uncomfortable for her to drive even if the weather was clear, never mind in this blizzard. By the time they reached the motorway Mac was able to increase his speed to thirty miles an hour. The slip road was closed and they had to continue to the next turn-off then head towards Dunblane to get home.

'God, will we ever get out if we go back to the cottage?'

Mac glanced at her. 'It hasn't been this heavy for years, but we've got more sophisticated gear these days, so the main roads will be kept clear.'

'Even the Rav is struggling in this. I wonder if there's a garage in the village with snow chains?'

'You must be kidding. Even if they had them they'll be long gone by now. The tyres on this are good. It's just too deep in the drifts to risk getting stuck.'

Viv's phone vibrated and another email arrived from Hahn. A row of smiley emojis with tears pouring from their eyes. No other words but another video attached. She passed it to Mac. 'It's too small to see it properly on that screen. Can't we trace his phone?'

Mac said, 'We'll be back in five minutes and be able to view it better. I will call in a favour. See if we can trace it.'

'I can do it, but the software I need is in Edinburgh.'

'I'll see what I can wangle.'

Doune was picture perfect, draped in white; the Catholic Church, perched up on the left, looked like a scene from a Christmas card.

Mac said, 'I think we'll leave the Rav at the end of the lane.'

'I wouldn't worry about the Rav's performance.'

'I'm not. I just don't want to block Mand in.'

Viv clocked a dark blue car with its engine labouring parked outside the gift shop.

They jumped out and trudged through the snow, which was easing slightly, towards the cottage. A single set of footprints preceded them all the way to the front door. As they approached, Ruddy stepped out from the porch and Moll started barking.

Ruddy said, 'She wouldn't let me in. Glad you've arrived sooner rather than later. Every time I stamped my feet to keep warm the dog went mad. Besides there's only so much stamping a man can do.'

Viv tapped at the door and shouted, 'Mand. Time to open up.'

Seconds later her sister appeared with James on her hip and undid the locks. 'Better safe than sorry,' Viv said, for the benefit of both Ruddy and Mand. Everyone took off their jackets and after she'd made a fuss of Moll who was birling round and round with excitement Viv took the wet stuff through to the back porch, its under-floor heating specifically for drying outdoor kit.

Mand looked uncomfortable. 'I didn't know . . .'

Viv shook her head, 'It's fine.'

Mand said, 'Kettle's on. What shall I make?'

Ruddy shivered. 'Anything hot that I can wrap my hands around.' Mand flushed pink and looked away.

Viv put a finger in the air. 'I think Sal has hot chocolate.' She raked around in the larder and held a tin of Green and Blacks aloft. 'The very stuff.' She stroked James's hair. He leaned his head against his mum's shoulder, the two looking like a Victorian painting idealising motherhood. The reality was a sleepy wee boy with a thumb in his mouth easing the pain of teething.

Ruddy coughed. 'Time for a different approach.'

Viv turned round. 'Thank God. We need his mobile traced.' She stopped spooning chocolate powder into mugs and showed him the new video on her laptop. 'He wants to play now.'

'What makes you think that?'

Mac said, 'He'd definitely been at Cultybraggan. Obviously thinks he's being funny and left behind a blow-up doll underneath a blanket.'

Mand looked at Viv. 'Oh God, that's horrible.' She went over to her and laid a hand on her arm. 'Vivi, that must have . . .'

Viv nodded. 'It was. But it probably means she's still alive. We have to believe she's alive . . . Let's concentrate on the maps and hope he hasn't left the area.'

They huddled round Viv's laptop as they played and replayed his latest video of Viv's mum. Different grubby brick background and the sound was much harsher, but she was alive and holding up another newspaper. Her message, 'Instead of making a transfer could you put the money into a holdall, used ten pound notes.'

Ruddy said, 'Send it straight to me and I'll have it enhanced asap, that way we should be able to trace the phone. But tracing it is only useful if he's kept it. The last video he sent we couldn't trace. He's probably cleverer than we're giving him credit for.'

'What about a helicopter with heat sensors?'

Ruddy looked at her. 'I've thought of that, but we can't go up in this weather. The forecast is for it to stop by morning. But that still means a whole lot of snow and if it freezes they won't fly either.'

'But mountain rescue fly in all weathers.'

He nodded. 'If we had evidence that she was injured . . .'

'We don't have evidence that she's not. She doesn't get to move. He might have broken her legs for all you know.'

'She doesn't look as if she's in pain. She's a pro, Viv. She knows what to do. She'll wait it out. Wear him down.'

'We can't assume she has the energy to wear him down. He's a strong man who was able to pull one over on me.' Her voice was desperate. She knew that there was protocol to follow if technical intervention was required, but she couldn't bear the sight of her mum staring blandly at the camera. 'It's odd that he hasn't given a deadline, is it not?'

Mac said, 'He's probably convinced either by his own delusions or by your mum's wiles that he will actually receive the money. If he doubted it he'd be more aggressive.'

'You'd think he'd just want to get hold of the money and get out.'

Viv caught a look passing between Mac and Ruddy.

'What? What's with the look?

Ruddy said, 'It depends on what he knows about your mum and . . .'

'And?'

'And her relationship with his own mother.'

'What are you not telling me?'

Ruddy glanced at Mac, 'Greta was in love with your mother. Some might say obsessed.'

Viv rubbed her face hard. 'But how did that happen? How did they know each other?'

Ruddy cleared his throat. 'Your mother was assigned to Greta's case. She was kind to her. Greta misinterpreted the signs. She must have. Your mother did her job exceptionally well. Have you heard of the term "swallow"?'

Viv screwed up her eyes. 'Yes. Mac mentioned, it's an old term for a female agent who . . . oh my God. My mum?' She rubbed her face again. 'Could this get any worse? So she was employed to seduce Greta.' She could barely get the name out. 'And then what?'

Ruddy said, 'Then things changed. There was someone that we needed to bring home and we'd got as much out of Greta as we were going to, so she was swapped.'

Mand gasped and shook her head.

Viv was no slouch on the Cold War, but she was having a difficult time getting her head round her mum's involvement in this cloak and dagger stuff – her mum seducing a woman, a spy, from another country in order to pump information out of her. She looked at Mac. 'Christ, Mac, try and imagine if this had been your mum. It just seems too outlandish. So improbable . . . and yet the more you tell me, the more . . .'

Mand said, 'It can't be true. Mum would never do that. She's always been . . .'

Viv and Mand stared at each other.

Viv said, 'I'm guessing you know this because you've read her files?'

Ruddy nodded. 'I wouldn't just make it up.'

Viv snorted, 'Oh please . . . if it was in your interest you'd have no problem making anything up. You'd tell us she was the tooth fairy if you thought you'd get away with it.'

Ruddy shook his head and glared at her. 'No, I certainly wouldn't. Your mother is a loyal colleague.'

'But she's not any more, is she. She's retired.'

'You don't get it, Viv. Once in the "family" . . .'

She interrupted him, 'I know, "always in the 'Family'".'

Mand said, 'What exactly is it that you do for them?' She gestured with her head to Ruddy and Mac, her face contorted with confusion.

Ruddy stared at Viv and made a tiny movement with his head.

She said to Mand, 'Not much, and nothing that you need to know about.'

'You've said that before. Surely I deserve some idea.'

With perfect timing Mac's phone rang and he strolled off to answer it. The moment passed and Mand made for the stairs, stroking James's head.

Ruddy said, 'You're doing a good job. We'll find them. But no one is going anywhere in this weather.'

Viv was about to object when he continued, 'I've got some film footage for you to go through.'

She was going to object again, but he put his hand up. 'It's CCTV footage from farmers in the area.'

She said, 'Since when did farmers have cameras in their yards?'

'Since a spate of agri thefts. Machines, tractors and for one guy a whole flock of sheep. Lifted in the night. So now lots of them have CCTV, some of it hooked up to police. Not all of it very good quality, but if you see anything that's useful we'll have it enhanced if need be. That should keep you busy for a bit.'

She wasn't convinced and walked over to the window to check what was going on with the snow. It was nowhere near as heavy, but still fluttering down. 'It's not so bad out there.' She turned and he handed her a USB stick.

'Get a look at that. He thinks he's invisible, but he's not. It might save you going up another blind alley.'

It made sense, but she still didn't want to stay put. He didn't move and kept his eyes on her. It wasn't an order, but she knew she was on the edge of being insubordinate. She sighed, 'Okay. I'll do it.'

'Good decision.'

Mac came back and stood with his hands on his hips. Ruddy tipped his head slightly to one side, questioningly.

Mac said, 'There's a situation at Fettes.'

Ruddy raised his wayward brows. 'What kind of situation?'

Mac glanced from Ruddy to Viv.

She said, 'For fuck sake! What is wrong with you guys?'

'The officer that we thought was going quietly has changed his mind. He's turned up at HQ armed.'

Ruddy said quickly, 'My driver is waiting on Main Street. Let's go.' He turned at the door. 'I know you'll be meticulous with the CCTV, I wouldn't expect anything less.'

Mac looked at her. 'Don't try anything. This incident at HQ might be over before we get there. I'll be back as soon as.' He stepped out into the silent night and closed the door.

Molly skirted round Viv's legs and nosed her hand, demanding attention. Viv kneeled down, snuggled into her neck and rubbed her ears. 'Poor baby, you could do with some TLC. Come.' She patted her thigh and Moll trotted at her side into the conservatory, where Viv stuck the USB in. She patted the couch and Moll hesitated, but jumped up and curled in beside her, pushing her head between Viv's stomach and the laptop.

'Oh, it's like that, is it?'

Moll didn't shift, so Viv stroked her head then got down to her search. The footage went back five days. That was a lot of footage. She knew 99.9 per cent of it would be mind-numbingly dull, but that was the nature of the work, for the 0.1per cent that could be gold. Fingers crossed. After the first few minutes of searching she had a whole new view of what farmers did. She had no idea that they were up and out in what was the middle of the night for the rest of the country. Good grief, four am was no time in the winter to have to get out of a cosy bed day after day to feed your cows, but these farmers did. They were also still working at ten and eleven o'clock at night, checking livestock or whatever else needed locking up. She guessed that since the thefts the rhythm of their days would be spoiled by the tension of not knowing whether your herd would still be there in the morning. Eventually, as she was losing the will to live, she spotted a black pick-up, too shiny to be a farm vehicle. She stopped the tape and enlarged the frame. There were two people in the front and one of them was not her mum. She went back online to check Kurt Hahn's concert dates and saw that they had been cancelled. 'Shit! So they are in it together.' She wrote down the time and exact frame the pick-up appeared in then rubbed her face before continuing the minute by minute search. The next time the vehicle showed up was earlier that afternoon. It seemed that she and Mac had missed him on the back road to Crieff. She needed more footage closer to the camp. She heard James crying upstairs, but kept her head down and began a new search. She didn't hear Mand approaching until she spoke.

'I made a veggie bake earlier. You must be starving.'

Viv wanted to get on with what she was doing, but knew her sister was swallowing her pride. 'Okay, great.' She snapped the laptop shut and wandered behind Mand to the kitchen.

'No news of Sal?' Mand asked.

Viv shook her head, 'Only the first day she arrived. I guess they're getting their money's worth.'

'What exactly is it she does?'

Viv shrugged. 'Good question. Sometimes it beats me. She does psychological profiling, but seems to have other strings to her bow. She helped to design facial recognition software and now she's hanging out with FBI for a "sabbatical".'

'D'you think she'll be all right with us being here for so long?'

'Of course. You couldn't find a more generous woman. In fact, she'd be offended if we didn't, so we're totally covered.'

Mand pulled out the bake from the Aga, and as soon as the smell hit Viv she realised just how hungry she was. 'Smells fantastic, what's in it?'

'Oh, this and that. Courgettes, aubergines, onions, tomatoes and a few herby things that I found in the larder.'

'Is James asleep?'

Mand nodded. 'Poor wee chap is out of his routine.'

It hadn't occurred to Viv that her sister now lived by a toddler's routine, but why wouldn't she?

They sat opposite each other and ate in silence for the first few bites, then Mand said, 'She is strong. I know she is, but I still think all of this will push her to, or beyond her limits.'

Viv said, 'It is so weird, you know, thinking that you've had one kind of mum, then finding out she wasn't that person at all. The thing is I've always thought she was a great mum. We were disciplined and guided, fed well. I've got good family memories of holidays, family gatherings with you, mum and dad and grannie. There was nothing odd about it. No whispers in the street or from our pals' parents at the school gate. She's brilliant to have juggled all that without us feeling deprived of her.'

'Dad was the one I wanted more of, but I don't know many people who, if they'd had a dad like ours, wouldn't say the same thing.'

Viv pointed at her plate with her fork. 'Where did you learn to cook like this? It's delicious.' She couldn't make eye contact with Mand for fear of welling up. They'd never talked about their dad. The family, what was left of them, had a tacit agreement not to go there, but one day they'd have to. Viv was conscious of how much the pain of losing her dad affected her every day, especially how it influenced the special jobs that Ruddy provided her with. At some level her determination to bring others to justice meant she would gain justice for what happened to him. At another level she knew that this wasn't true at all, but was consoled by the lie. They finished their food.

Mand said, 'I feel useless. I can't do anything. I've got to be with James.'

'Of course you do. No one expects you to go out hunting for her. Just think how delighted she'll be when she gets home and sees James' glorious wee face.'

'You think she'll come home?'

Viv nodded. 'Yes I do. I can't pretend I'm not worried about what state she'll be in, but his trick with the doll makes me think he's not a killer. He's a desperate man and they are unpredictable, but he knows that without her alive there's no deal with the dosh. His only chance of seeing it is if she is returned alive.' She screwed up her eyes. 'Actually it's odd that he hasn't given us a drop point. Maybe now that the weather is bad he'll change his mind about prolonging the game. Fingers crossed, but don't you worry about not being able to help. I'm telling you that nosh was brilliant. When I'm wound up I forget to eat.'

She stood, lifted both their empty plates and took them to the dishwasher and stacked them inside. 'I'll carry on looking at the CCTV footage. There's more than one person in the pick-up and I don't think it's mum.'

'Does that make mum's chances of escaping more difficult?'

Viv shrugged. 'No idea whether the brothers are in this together or not. Best case scenario would be that the pianist is trying to reason with his brother.' This sounded weak and she knew it. 'We'll see.'

She went back to her laptop and continued her search. Each camera had its own file and it was a laborious task scanning through them. Occasionally she'd get another false alarm, but by the final file she'd only had that one sighting. The strath that ran between Dunblane and Perth was huge and was divided into large agricultural units, mostly pasture for sheep, cattle or both.

From the view on Google Maps most farms had massive sheds, no doubt to house their livestock in bad weather, like now. It wasn't outwith the bounds of reason that he could be using one of them, but it was unlikely since the farmers were active. Then she homed in on one farm that looked derelict. She'd been so focused on the military buildings she'd overlooked the fact that any building would do. She scratched her head, irritated with herself for not thinking about this sooner. The last file on the USB came from a camera directed on a farm track that edged a spruce plantation. It was like watching slow TV as snow blew and swirled then eventually built up along the edge of the plantation. Finally she rubbed her eyes then started as a set of headlights came into frame. She slowed the film right down and stared as a black pick-up edged along the track. It stopped and Kristian Hahn got out. What the heck was he doing? She could only see the top of his head as he faced the trees. He must be taking a leak. She couldn't help herself snorting, imagining the irony of his body parts freezing off in the process. He jumped back inside and drove on. She couldn't make out who was in the truck and cursed that she hadn't got the software to properly enhance it. She thought of sending it back to Ruddy then remembered he had his own issue to deal with. What the hell. She'd send it anyway. Surely he had a PA who could do it? She did have somewhere else she could pack it off to, but decided that the most important thing was that she now had a date, time and sighting of at least one Hahn. She checked the weather forecast. The heaviest snow was over, but the threat of it freezing was high, meaning that driving anywhere but the main roads would continue to be difficult. On the up side if she did find his tyre tracks there was less chance of anyone else having been over them. Worth a look.

She went upstairs and tapped gently on Mand's bedroom door. 'Mand, I need to go out for a bit. Could you lock up again?'

Mand opened the door and put her finger to her lip. 'He's not yet sound asleep.' She walked to the top of the stairs. 'Where are you going? I don't want you to do anything stupid.'

Viv bristled, but knew what she meant. 'I'm not planning to do anything stupid, but I've found a track where he was. I think it's worth checking.' She looked at her watch. 'I'm going to go off my head if I just hang about here all night.'

'Yeah, you might, but I'll go off mine knowing that you are out there on your own in the pitch dark. You'll just have to stick it out until Mac gets back.'

Viv was about to object, but the look on Mand's face told her there was no arguing. She bit the inside of her lip and nodded. 'I'll go over the tapes again in case I've missed something. You head off to bed. It's been a long day.'

'You think I came up the Clyde in a banana boat? There's no way I'm going to sleep until you do. So how about you go to bed. If it's been a long day for me it's been even longer for you . . . You're doing your best, Viv. You don't have to be superwoman.'

Aware of her irritation rising Viv said, 'Okay, I'll wait for Mac to get back.'

Mand shook her head. 'You're such a bad liar. I can see from your face that you have no intention of waiting for Mac. You're just palming me off with a story so that I'll hit the hay and you can sneak off and do your thing.

I don't want to lose two people I . . .' she choked back the words and retreated to her bedroom.

Viv's phone vibrated. Surprised to see Sal's number she rushed down to the conservatory so that her conversation wouldn't wake James.

'Sal! How the hell are you? I've been dying for you to ring.' This wasn't quite true but close enough.

The voice that spoke wasn't Sal's, but another woman's. 'Oh, I pressed the wrong number by mistake.' The call ended and Viv was left with echoes of an American accent lingering in her ears. Why was someone else using Sal's phone? Who was she? She pressed to return the call, but it went straight to voice mail. What was going on? Exasperated she rubbed her hands through her hair. The last thing she needed was to worry about Sal, but at least she could be thankful for the small mercy that the bump on her head was no longer as tender. She dumped herself onto the couch with her laptop and revisited the CCTV. She couldn't concentrate and went back over each frame two or three times before finding a rhythm. Her phone vibrated again. This time it was Mac's number.

'Hi. Have you sorted out the . . .'

He interrupted her, 'He shot himself.'

Viv gasped, 'My God, so what happens now?'

'Damage limitation. It all took place inside Fettes, but that's a double-edged sword. Whatever way we release this to the press they'll have a field day. We'll be here for at least another hour then I'll get back up the road.'

'Will you come straight here?'

'I wasn't planning on that. I need to get some shut-eye. Why, what have you found?'

She gave him the info about Hahn's last sighting on the CCTV and said, 'I think it's worth taking a look. There won't be much, if any traffic along that track.'

He interrupted, 'Look, let me get a couple of hours' sleep and then we'll both take a look.'

She was itching to get going, but this was as good as she was going to get. 'Okay. What time will I set my alarm for?'

'Six.'

She drew in a breath, about to object, but he continued.

'Just in case I get stuck here longer than I think I will.'

It made sense, but still, if it was his mum . . . he'd probably do exactly the same thing.

She said, 'Fine.'

'Viv, even at six it'll be pitch dark.'

'I know, but what if it snows again. We'll lose any tracks that . . .' She was on a hiding to nothing. 'Okay, okay. Here at six then.' She wanted to add 'sharp', but Mac was as much a stickler for punctuality as she was.

'Right you are.'

She shook her head. That was the kind of thing her mum would have said.

Chapter Fifteen

Tuesday

True to form Mac's 4x4 approached at one minute to six. Viv had been out for a short run with Moll who'd objected to being woken at such an ungodly hour, but once she was out had embraced the snow like a puppy. The ground was frozen and it was hard to break through the skin of ice that had formed over the powdery snow, but she'd needed at least fifteen minutes across the river park to release her trapped adrenaline. Feeling refreshed she made porridge and coffee, expecting that Mac wouldn't have had breakfast. An extra ten minutes wouldn't matter now.

Molly greeted him at the door like a long-awaited friend, which Viv realised he probably was. She beckoned him through to the kitchen, pointing above, 'Mand and James haven't stirred yet.'

He said, 'Not many do at this hour.'

She placed two bowls of porridge on the table and poured out mugs of steaming coffee. 'Here, fortify yourself. I bet you haven't eaten.'

'Nope.' He rubbed his hands across his face. 'What a night. Got three hours in the end. This looks great.' He drew a chair up and they ate in silence.

Eventually he murmured, 'I understand why this is a national dish.'

'Mum used to tell us it would put hairs on our chest. Imagine, as if two daughters would want that.'

Viv put the empty bowls and mugs in the dishwasher and they both kitted up. 'It's Baltic out there.'

'I know. My cottage is almost a thousand feet above sea level. Colder than here.'

'It's not a competition. I was just saying so that you'd wrap up.'

'Why thank you for your concern.'

'Sarc will get you everywhere. C'mon, let's find my mum.'

'It's odd that he hasn't sent a drop-off time.'

'Agreed, but I don't think he's in this alone. The CCTV showed two males in the front of the truck and I checked Kurt's concerts again. They'd been cancelled. Facebook is a wonderful thing when people are aggrieved.' She grinned. 'There's no way to keep that kind of thing quiet these days. He thinks we're amateurs. First rule of conflict, "Know thine enemy". He hasn't done his homework.'

'Don't tempt fate.'

They walked into the village ankle deep in snow, to where they'd left the Rav. The main roads where clear and Doune was shrouded in that silence that only comes with snow. Once in the car Viv showed Mac on a road map the position where the last sighting of Hahn had been. It only took them ten minutes on the motorway to reach the turn-off but at the top of the slip road the surface remained untouched by a plough and they had to slow to a crawl again. Compacted tracks had turned into an ice rink. Even the Rav struggled to stay in a straight line.

Mac stayed in as high a gear as he could, but the wheels spun and they veered off the centre of the road towards the ditch. Viv covered her eyes, unable to believe that the weather could hamper their progress this early in the search. Mac managed to steer into the skid and they remained on the hard surface.

'Phew. Well done. I'm never sure what to do, but instinctively always hit the brake.' Her phone vibrated. 'Early bird.' She fished around in her jacket pocket and hauled it out. Sal's number again. Before she answered it stopped vibrating. Odd. She tucked it back into her jacket. She'd deal with Sal later. For now they had to keep on the look-out for landmarks that would give access to the track at the back of the spruce plantation. It had looked as if there were two options on the map. One through a farmyard, round a field then onto what must be a track otherwise he wouldn't have driven it.

She glanced at Mac. 'It might not be a track at all. I've just assumed it was because he was on it. But a pick-up has much higher clearance even than the Rav.'

'Only one way to find out. But we've got to locate the farm first. Then worry about whether there's a track or not.'

They drove along a straight stretch lined with high, but mixed planting, branches heavy with snow caught in the headlights. 'These mono-plantations only have a thirty- or forty-year cycle. Forests marked on this map may no longer be here.'

He slowed to stop. 'Look at this.' He pointed to a long straight road. 'Roman. Still there to this day. Don't look at features that man can interfere with. Roads can change but are less likely to. Streams and rivers, crossing points usually chosen because it's the point of least resistance, easiest or narrowest.' He drove on.

'I'm not daft. I was just saying about the mono-plantations because they're planted specifically to be harvested.'

Mac said, 'Here, what about this place?'

On the right the plantation ended and a field edged with post and rail fencing came into view. The headlights flickered over a wooden stable with a Shetland pony munching on a net full of hay hanging outside its door. A turn-off at the end of the field led towards a farm.

'This is it.' Viv looked at the map, then at Mac. 'What will we say if the farmer is about?'

'We'll tell him the truth. We're looking for a black pick-up.'

'That's lame. And by the way the farmer could be a woman.' He ignored the jibe and she continued, 'You any idea how many black pick-ups were rented or sold in the last three months?'

'No, but I get the feeling I will soon.'

'Plenty. Most of them Nissans, like the one we're after.' Her phone vibrated again. She hesitated. If it was Sal's number she wouldn't answer anyway. It wasn't; it was a text message. 'Time to deliver the money', she held it up for Mac to see. 'It was sent yesterday. It's been sitting on a server somewhere. He sent it at nine-thirty last night. What shall we do? There's an address. Gloagburn café at ten-thirty am.'

Mac shrugged, 'Never heard of it, have you?' She shook her head.

He continued, 'Besides we don't have the money. Maybe we can call his bluff.'

'I've got a sports bag in the boot. Got some stinky running kit in there but . . .'

'You think we should about turn? Get some dosh and see if he'll bite?'

'The bank doesn't open until nine-thirty and by the time we do that . . . oh God. Let's think this through. We can probably come up with enough money to make it look like £500,000.'

Mac said, 'I've got an idea.' He pulled into the farm entrance and took out his phone. 'He's not going to thank me for ringing at this hour but needs must.' He let the number ring and ring then just as he was about to cut the call a voice bellowed out from the speaker. Mac held the phone away from his ear and grinned. 'Viv's had another message from our kidnapper.'

It was disturbing to hear him called that, but it's exactly what he was.

Mac continued, 'He's sent us a drop-off place and time. I thought we could get the bank to issue the amount in recalled ten pound notes. That way they'd be of no value if he did manage to take off.'

Viv couldn't hear the rest of the conversation from the other end, but Mac made noises of acceptance and it sounded as if his idea was possible, with a couple of calls by Ruddy to the right people. Finally Mac said, 'We can get to Dunblane in . . .'

Ruddy obviously interrupted, wasn't concerned that Mac could get to a bank and agreed to make the calls.

'So what now?'

She said, 'We might as well take a look since we've come this far.'

'Okay, your call.'

They drove through the large farmyard where there was evidence of lots of vehicle movement. On the left a dark green modern shed housed cattle. They were already feeding, their heads protruding through metal rails and munching from a trough that was almost full. The farmer must have been around very recently, but there was no sign of anyone now. Viv opened her window, but rapidly shut it again. 'Wow, what a stink. I suppose you get used to it when you've got it day in day out.'

Mac grinned. 'A country girl you are not.'

'Well, that should be no surprise to you who've known me for . . . ever. Always loved the feeling of tarmac beneath my feet. Never been a fan of anything squelchy.'

He raised his eyebrows. She play-punched his upper arm. 'You!'

A modern farmhouse, with lights on in the downstairs rooms, stood at the furthest point on the yard away from the road. The roof of the two-storey villa was topped with photovoltaic panels, its plain white pebbledash exterior a sign that it was built for purpose not aesthetics. A flat area to one side with a sagging washing line seemed to confirm this.

Mac said, 'Always an early start for these guys. Unsung heroes. I mean where would we all be without them? I wouldn't make a habit of getting up at five or six in the morning. And I don't even need to ask if you would?'

'There.' She pointed, 'There's a gap between those small barns.'

Mac drove the Rav towards it. Another vehicle had already been there. He turned his wheels to drive through but noticed, in the rearview mirror, the door to the house open and a man come out tucking his trousers into boots and shrugging into a jacket. He marched towards them, scowling like the proverbial grumpy Farmer Jack as he pulled on a cap.

'What do you think you're up to?' he growled at them.

Mac didn't waste any time and pulled out his ID. He lowered his window and held it up.

'That's all well and good, but doesn't explain why you're here.'

Mac said, 'We're looking for a black pick-up.'

The man stepped back slightly, 'Why? What's he done?'

'It's complicated, but if you've seen him where would we find him?'

The farmer pointed to the house. 'He's in his bed. No chance of him being up before daylight.'

'I think we're talking at cross purposes.'

'My boy drives a black pick-up.'

'Nissan?' Viv asked.

The farmer didn't look at her. 'No, his is a Mitsubishi.'

'So, have you seen another pick-up around?'

The farmer removed his cap and scratched his head. 'Can't say I have.'

'Not heard anything in the night?' Viv said.

Again he replied to Mac. 'Well, that's a different question. I have heard someone in the night, but they didn't stop in the yard; they went along behind the wood.'

Viv again. 'Did you follow them?'

'No.' He turned and gestured with his head. 'There's a way out about a mile further on. There's a development of houses on the old military site. There's nothing to steal between me and the building site. There used to be pheasant in the pen at the end of the wood but not now.'

Mac said, 'You mind if we take a look then?'

'On you go. There hasn't been anyone at the development for weeks. Think they've run out of cash.' He gave a hint of a smile, as if he was relaxing.

They were about to go on their way and his son was in the clear, so why wouldn't he relax?

The Rav had no difficulty on snow that hadn't been compacted and they bumped their way along the side of the wood. Viv pointed to a spot ahead. 'Here. I think this is where he got out to take a leak.'

Sure enough, a luminous patch of yellow as yet not re-covered by snow. There was nothing else to see until a little further on they spotted an area where the lower branches of the trees had been removed and stacked into A-shaped hides. Presumably this was the pheasant pen. At the end of the wood they were in open countryside, with unsullied white fields on either side but no sign of a development. Another half mile on and the top of an industrial cement mixer came into view, followed by the ubiquitous blue panels of unfinished buildings sitting in a dip that couldn't be seen from the farm. Right in the middle of the development stood a concrete wartime pill box. The side facing them was covered in black graffiti. Mac glanced at Viv who was chewing her lip. Once they reached the site they could see where the tracks had stopped. There were multiple footprints on both sides of the ruts, so two people had got out. The driver had walked round and then back. The activity was confusing; prints over prints over prints. Not easy to decipher. But the tyre tracks then continued.

Viv hissed, 'Shit!'

'We still have a track to follow.'

'Yes, but they've been here then gone . . . somewhere else.'

They jumped out of the Rav and walked to the entrance. A rusty metal door easy to open, another corridor with water dripping in through the roof, so not as well built as the other bunkers. Viv switched on her phone torch and they continued inside. It was a smaller space but still with rooms marked Radio control room, Boiler room, Dry store and Toilet, off to one side.

'So this was for radio communication, not for saving the great and the good of a community?'

'It doesn't feel as if they actually spent any time here.'

'They couldn't. Must just have done a recce and decided it was too wet . . . We can but hope.'

'Imagine if you were him. You'd no more want to spend your nights in a freezing bunker than fly to the moon. I wonder if he's ended up using the pick-up?'

She shrugged. 'It's possible, but maybe too cosy. Let's get to Dunblane and gather the cash. We've got a date to keep.'

'There's no guarantee that the bank will do it.'

'Don't underestimate Ruddy.'

'I don't, but there'll be all sorts of legal loopholes to get through, and probably a JP involved. All takes time.'

Viv's belly contracted. 'Ruddy will make it happen.'

Mac glanced at her. 'You do know he's human, right?'

She ignored him. Since Ruddy had known both of her parents they were definitely 'family' to him. He'd pull out every stop possible to make it happen. She had to believe that. The development's exit was on a narrow B road, but within a quarter of a mile they were on to an A route which was only four miles from the motorway.

Mac had to do a dodgy right turn across the motorway but at that time of the day there was still very little traffic. The snow was both a godsend and a hassle. The ploughs had been out and cleared both lanes so the journey back was effortless. Doune was still and quiet but with a few more lights on in houses.

Molly barked as they walked to the front door.

'That'll be Mand and James awake now.'

She had no need to worry; they were already up and sitting at the kitchen table.

Mand looked questioningly at Viv.

Viv shook her head. 'No luck.'

Mac's phone rang and he did as he always did and took it outside.

When he returned he said, 'Let's get another look at those videos.'

Viv said, 'Why? Who was that?'

'One of the tech guys I sent them to. He has a theory.'

'Well, let's hear it then.'

'He thinks that the videos were made at the same time and that the newspapers are fake.'

'Shit! I should go with my instinct. When I saw them I got a funny feeling in my gut, but just didn't pay attention to it.'

She ran the videos again. Between the two there was barely forty-five seconds of footage. The first was slightly longer than the second. 'He could have just moved her from one room to another, or out into the corridor. Bastard!'

'The second bit sounds different, but it could just be down to the absence of carpet on the floor.'

Viv checked the *Scotsman*'s website for the headlines of the days he'd posted. Both were different from the real front pages. She pulled at her hair and yelled. James flinched and his lip trembled. 'Oh, I'm so sorry, I didn't mean to scare . . .'

Mand glared at her, scooped James up and shushed him back to peace.

'So where does that leave us? If the videos were taken on the first day, Sunday, then we haven't seen her for two whole days.'

Mac's phone rang again.

Viv paced round the kitchen trying to make sense of why he would do that. To take two videos at the same time was premeditating something, but what? What had he planned? And had he done whatever he wanted to?

Mac returned. 'You'll never believe this.'

'Try me.'

'He's left the country. Got on a flight to Berlin at six-thirty this morning.'

'How can he? How can that be?'

The timing was unbelievably tight.

'Who was that?'

'The boss, Ruddy. He'd put out an alert at Scottish airports. The pick-up was returned and . . . doesn't matter about the how, but he'll be questioned at the other end by German police.'

'D'you think he came with a return flight expecting to be here for three or four days? Totally unbelievable. What has he done with her?'

'The pick-up is being impounded, so at least we've got that before it's been cleaned. There'll be evidence inside. Always a trace of something.' He walked into the conservatory and stared out. 'I don't know why, but I don't think he's . . .'

'Don't say it. It's like tempting fate. So what about that café? That was just an additional wild goose chase. We should go now. He might have dumped her there.'

Mac already had a map up on his phone, looking at the route between where they'd been this morning already and the café, and how long it was from the café to the airport. 'It's possible. Look.' He traced the route with his finger as Viv tracked it.

'Okay, let's get back out there. We still don't know what we'll find. Mand, I'm sorry I yelled. Is he okay?'

Mand said, 'He's fine. Life's pretty quiet with only two of us. Take care out there. This guy's a trickster.'

Mac drove back the same way they'd just been. 'Wondering about the brother.'

'Me too. I wonder if he turned up to help or to . . . oh, God knows. This is mad. His return home means one of two things. Either he got what he came for or he didn't. I have to hope that he didn't and that she's okay.'

'It hasn't occurred to you . . .'

'Most things have occurred to me, but I can't bear to think of them.'

Once off the motorway the road hadn't been cleared, so their journey to the café was pretty hairy on compacted snow. Dawn was edging its way up across the eastern horizon, but there were still few vehicles about. There were half a dozen cars in the car park and the place was lit up like a beacon. A sign on the door said 'Closed', so they knocked on the glass. Music on inside was evidence of life.

Mac knocked harder. 'Wait here, I'll go round the back.'

Within seconds someone approached the door from inside and let her in. Mac was in the kitchen already, questioning the cook.

He was nodding as Viv approached. 'What time was this?'

'Oh, we've only been in for an hour and a half. She was at the door when we arrived.'

The smell of fried onions and home baking intermingled, and the cook wiped her brow with the back of her hand.

Mac continued, 'And you say she made a phone call?'

The cook nodded. 'Yes. Said her battery had gone flat and could she use the phone, and she did.'

'Then what?'

'Someone came to pick her up.'

Viv said, 'What was he like?'

'Not sure, didn't see.'

Mac said, 'Driving an old Land Rover?'

'I didn't see . . . she was in a bit of a mess.'

Viv drew in breath. 'D'you mean she was hurt or just grubby?'

'Oh, she was hurt. But wouldn't hear of us helping.'

Viv marched back out to the Rav, but had to wait a few minutes before Mac came out.

'Find out anything more?'

'Not really. But why . . .' He left the question hanging.

'Only one way to find out. Let's go speak to the Colonel.'

The route back to Doune was busier now and the sun was up. Snow already showed signs of melting, car tracks were turning to slush, and a salty shower from lorries sprayed over the windscreen. The track up to the Colonel's house was even more precarious than last time; it was as if the camber had been designed by a slalom expert. The Rav slid this way and that on hard snow. No luck on the melting here. By some fluke Mac managed to keep them out of the ditch. They backed into his drive blocking in the Colonel's car. Mac jumped out, went to the Land Rover and laid his hand on the bonnet; warm.

The Colonel came to the door and said, 'Any luck yet?'

This was not what Viv wanted to hear. 'We were hoping you'd be able to tell us.'

His brows knitted in confusion. 'I haven't heard from her. What makes you think I would have?'

Viv glared at him. Was he telling the truth or just a fabulous liar?

Mac said, 'Been out already this morning?'

The Colonel nodded. 'Of course. I've been to the village for my newspaper.' He beckoned them in. Same routine as last time, with the dogs hugging their beds by the Aga until they absolutely had to get up and greet the new arrivals. A few sniffs and they retreated. Viv could understand why. She could see her breath ahead of her in the kitchen. If this was the heart of the home she'd hate to think what the rest of the house felt like. The *Times* was open on the table. At the obits page she noticed. What was it with old people and obituaries? Desperate to be the last man standing? She checked the date. He was telling the truth.

Her mind reeled at the possibilities of who else her mum would ring. As the obituaries pages would testify, her circle of friends had diminished.

A strange sensation in her belly made her spin round to Mac. 'I think I've got it.' She strode outside and made a call. 'Is she with you?'

Ruddy answered in the affirmative. 'She doesn't want to be seen.'

'But she's my mum.'

'I know that, but she probably rang me because she didn't want to alarm you.'

'Christ, it's way too late for that. What the hell has been going on? This has nothing to do with money, does it?'

'We'll talk about it soon enough, but for now she's safe and in good hands.'

'Whose hands?'

He sighed. 'I promised I wouldn't tell you where she was, so I have to keep that promise. But she's seen a doctor and . . .'

'But we have a right to know.'

He said, 'All in good time. You'll get the full story in good time.'

Viv stomped back inside and gestured to Mac with her head. 'Let's go.'

Mac came out behind her and started up the Rav's engine, 'Okay, spill.'

'She's with Ruddy. This whole thing has been a total wild fucking goose chase and some. He won't tell me anything yet, but she's in a bad way. I think she's been taken to hospital. What have I missed? This is about something that we don't know about. Have we been pawns?'

Mac said, 'It's unlikely. But if we have been it'll have been for good reason.'

'Not all reasons are good enough reasons. Look at the state Mand's been in. Look at me. I've been a wreck. Oh, my God, it had better be good.'

'Or what? You'll just have to swallow it, Viv. If she went to Ruddy my guess would be that she's got information for him.'

'D'you think this whole thing has been about information gathering? What could he have that is so important to us? By us I mean the UK.' She chewed on the inside of her cheek and was silent for the rest of the journey.

Mac pulled up outside the village shop. 'I think we need milk.' He slammed the door and she watched as he sauntered along the pavement.

Whatever Ruddy needed, he'd taken a huge risk using her mum. So to take that kind of risk would mean something to do with the dreaded National Security. She racked her brain, trawling its depths for something in Kristian's background. Her mind hooked the image of the flag on his Facebook profile. But what about his debt? Maybe it had nothing to do with debt, but something to do with politics. Mac appeared with milk, a bag of floury rolls, and a pack of bacon.

'Thought we could use some sustenance. Been a while since breakfast.' He grinned. 'Good result, no?'

She couldn't work out whether he was talking about potential bacon rolls or the fact that her mum was safe.

She scratched her head. 'I think I've been barking up the wrong tree.'

He interrupted her, 'Whatever tree you've been barking up you've done it because you believed it was the right one. You weren't doing it for the good of your health.'

'I think it might be to do with politics. He had a photograph of a flag on his Facebook profile. Far right, fascist shit. Why didn't I do more with that?'

'Because in the video she asked for money. How could you have known? I didn't know. I was with you on the money thing.'

They risked driving the Rav right up to the door. No longer worried about a quick getaway.

Mand opened up. 'Still no sign of her?' She ran her hands roughly into her hair and turned back into the cottage.

Viv said, 'She's safe.'

Mand spun round. 'How do you know?'

Viv plonked herself into a chair in the conservatory. 'I spoke to the man she's with.'

'What man? She's with that nut job.'

Viv stood and went to her sister, and for the first time in years hugged her. At first Mand was rigid, but Viv held on tight and Mand relaxed. Tears streamed down her face, which she swiped off with her sleeve. She said, 'Where is she? How come . . .'

'The only thing I know at the moment is that she's safe and in good hands.' Viv glanced at Mac for confirmation.

He nodded. 'We'll get the full story later. But the "nut job", as you say, has left the country and your mum contacted our boss who picked her up and has taken her to get . . .'

Viv shook her head to stop him from saying anything more.

'Bacon roll anyone?'

The sisters stared at him, then glanced at each other. Viv said, 'She'll be all right now.'

Mand said, 'Are you sure?'

'As sure as I can be. Let's make coffee. Where's James?'

'Asleep. He's exhausted.'

'He's not the only one. Boy, has she got some explaining to do.'

Mac whistled as he pottered around the Aga. 'I wouldn't bank on that. I've told you, she's old school.'

'If I hear one more thing about "old school", I think I'll kill someone. I want to see her and I want to see her right now. What does she think she's up to going to Ruddy and not us? She must know how worried we all are. One phone call. One sodding phone call would have been all it took.'

Mac said, 'Don't kid yourself. If she'd made one call to you there's no way you'd have let her off the hook. She called the boss because it was the wisest move. He'll have either brought in a doctor or taken her to our clinic.'

'What clinic? When I've been injured I've never been taken to "our clinic". Where is it?'

He continued frying bacon.

She thought of yelling, but with James upstairs asleep decided against. 'Can you take me to her?'

'No. Not unless she asks for visitors.'

'Why wouldn't she want to see us?'

'Think about it, Viv. She must be bruised or looks a mess and doesn't want to alarm you.'

'Enough with the "alarm me" shit. Trust me I'm alarmed. As alarmed as I could be that my mum choses to ring a stranger over me.'

'He's not exactly a stranger. When you . . .'

'Don't even think about saying calm down.'

He held up his hands in defence. 'Don't blame the messenger.'

'You're not the bloody messenger. You're supposed to be my friend.'

Mand said, 'Enough you two. It's like listening to an old married couple arguing.'

'He wishes!' Viv grabbed the dog's lead and went to the door. 'Come Moll, walkies.' She almost slammed the door but again remembered James just in time.

She waded about fifty feet across the field, hampered by snow a foot deep.

She stopped. Moll couldn't run because of the weight and size of snowballs gathering between her front legs. Viv stood and stared at Doune Castle, looming over the Ardoch burn, its magnificent curtain wall covered in scaffolding, an attempt to rescue the ancient structure from decay. How does anything survive? Moll sat at her feet and pawed her leg.

'Okay, let's go back.' She lifted the dog and carried her like a baby to the back door of the cottage, where Sal had a hosepipe for the very purpose of rinsing off the dog. Viv turned the tap but nothing came. Brian must have switched it off for the winter. She lifted the dog into the porch and tried to free her of the balls of ice. With soothing words one by one she picked off the balls and threw them back outside, until eventually Moll was back to normal. She towel dried her, all the time speaking to her as if she could understand.

Chapter Sixteen

'Right, I'm off to Edinburgh. No reason for us to stay here now.'

Mand and Mac sat at the kitchen table and munched into bacon rolls, ignoring Viv's snippy protestation.

Getting the message she went upstairs as quietly as possible and began to throw things into her rucksack. She pulled the duvet back and was about to strip it from the bed, but instead crawled under, and with her knees tucked into a foetal position she closed her eyes and allowed sleep to come. A tap on the door woke her with a start. She swung her legs over the side of the bed and rubbed her eyes. 'Come in.'

Mac stuck his head round the door. 'I've had a call. We can go and see her.'

'Right, I need to have a shower to wake myself up. Give me five.'

When she appeared in the kitchen it had been cleaned and Mand and James had their coats on ready to go.

Mand said, 'We're all packed. I've got mum's things in the car and I'll go straight to her flat.'

Viv, astonished at how much had been achieved while she slept, rubbed Mand's arm. 'Thanks for doing that.' She glanced around the immaculate kitchen. No evidence of all the activity of the previous few days.

'I've left the beds for you to deal with.'

'Sure, I'll be back to see Moll later. In fact I'll just ring Brian. Let him know we're decanting back to Edinburgh.'

She took off and made the call.

Mac said, 'No children allowed where we're going. In fact no civilians.' He glanced at Mand, who frowned but said nothing.

Viv said, 'I thought she was in a hospital. I mean like the Western General or something.'

He shook his head. 'No, she is in a clinic. You'll see when we get there. D'you want to go in one car? I'll leave the Audi here if you like.'

She hesitated. 'Okay. Let's get an update on the roads and weather.'

'I've already checked. Main roads are clear. No more snow forecast. Icy conditions coming, but not until tonight.'

'OK, let's get going then.'

Once they reached Edinburgh Viv drove back the same route she'd used for Fettes, but continued towards the Botanical Gardens and beyond to Dundas Street. Mac directed her to turn onto Northumberland Street, then up a lane heading south. She stopped outside what looked like a typical mews property, with a garage door at ground level and a suite of rooms above. Mac jumped out and rang a buzzer at the side of the building. The garage door opened automatically and he jumped back into the Rav.

She drove in and Mac opened his window then said, 'Switch the engine off.' He pressed a series of buttons on a panel and they began to move. Viv couldn't help herself from smiling.

'What the hell is this?'

'It's a lift taking us down to the lower level.'

He grinned. He enjoyed showing her new places. They reached their destination with the slightest of bumps. Another door opened and Mac gestured for her to drive out into a huge underground car park. Rows of dark coloured cars filled most of it. She backed into a space furthest away from the only door she could see. Mac sauntered to the door and laid a card against the sensor. It hissed aside and she followed him through. He knew his way around, so he'd clearly already been here before. She realised you would need special clearance to get in here. This was no concrete bunker built in a rush for dignitaries of the Cold War. It was built with state of the art materials, more like a corporate building. After a short, wide corridor Mac used his card again to open another door. She guessed top grade bullet-proof opaque glass and steel.

'This place is amazing. We must be walking beneath Abercrombie Place and . . .'

'Yeah, you guessed it. Queen Street Gardens.'

'Bloody hell. It's massive.'

He turned and grinned at her. 'Love it when I'm able to surprise you.'

'Well, you've succeeded. Look at me, how surprised am I? Totally. But is this where the clinic is?'

He nodded. 'It's only one part of the complex ,but yes it's where people from all over the country . . .'

She interrupted him. 'By people do you mean agents?'

'Yes, but there are also people who work in Intel who are not. So many different things to do these days. Anyway, there are always a few of us who need medical attention somewhere out of the public glare. Too difficult to explain if we were taken to an ordinary hospital.'

This made complete sense to her, but she'd been hurt a couple of times, needed the odd stitch or check-up, and never been brought here. 'How come I never made it here?'

'The public always saw or got wind of your involvement. If you'd been brought here too many questions would have been asked about your whereabouts. Your treatment in a public hospital kept this place under wraps. There's always someone following up on details. No one,' he glared at her 'and I mean no one can know about this place.' He gestured with his hands expansively.

'Spare me the histrionics.'

Finally they reached another entrance which took them into a space like a proper hospital reception. Polished tiled floors and the smell of antiseptic and cleanliness confirmed that they'd swapped one kind of officialdom for another.

Mac walked toward the desk holding up his card, which Viv thought unnecessary since they couldn't have got this far without one. A tall woman, with her hair scraped back into a ponytail, wearing scrubs, stood behind a high counter. She pointed to a door. 'They're expecting you.'

Mac knocked then pushed the door open. Viv's mum sat on a bed. Ruddy and a woman with a clipboard stood either side of her. They all looked round as Viv and Mac entered. Viv got a flicker of recognition from the woman, but couldn't remember where she'd seen her before.

Viv went to her mum, but an almost imperceptible movement of her eyes stopped Viv from hugging her. How quickly and subtly we receive these signals. Her mum took her hand and said, 'None of this was meant to hurt you.'

Viv, horrified, felt tears prick her eyes. This was no place for an emotional reunion. She squeezed her mum's hand and turned to Ruddy. 'Is there an explanation?'

He said, 'Always, but not usually what you want to hear.'

'Try me.'

The woman stepped forward and introduced herself as Dr Arbuthnott. 'Your mum's had a bit of a knock, but she'll survive.'

'What kind of "bit of a knock"?'

'Mainly bruising. Probably a cracked rib.'

'How come only probably? Surely an x-ray will show you?'

'She has an old injury and we can't tell whether the hairline fracture is new or not.'

'So you're saying she's had a cracked rib before?'

The doctor turned to Ruddy as if checking what more she could say.

He gave a tiny shake of his head. 'I'll take it from here.'

The doctor walked toward the door, but stopped right next to Viv. 'She's fine. I wouldn't mind being in that kind of shape now, never mind when I reach her age.' She touched Viv's arm and whispered, 'CC's.' A current ran between them and they stepped apart.

Viv said, 'What a strange place this is. How can people work without daylight?'

Her mum smiled and stretched her hand to Viv. 'That's my girl.'

Ruddy said, 'She can go home, but'll need meals on wheels for a bit.'

Her mum protested. 'I will not. I'm perfectly capable of putting something in the oven. I concede that I wouldn't mind a hand with some shopping though.'

Viv shook her head. 'Mand's already on it.'

Mac looked at Viv. 'Don't know why you're shaking your head. You'd do exactly the same. Won't let anyone help you.'

Viv began to protest, but he held up his hand, 'Don't pretend . . .'

She interrupted, 'I've let you help me. More than anyone else I know you've come to my rescue.' Mac had always been there for her; she mustn't take him for granted.

The door clicked closed as the doctor left.

Mac said to Ruddy, 'Is this about politics?'

'Everything is about politics, sometimes with a large P, sometimes with a small one. This episode was in danger of becoming the larger variety. But thanks to Trude we've got the information we needed and it's already been passed to . . .'

'And will we ever know who that is?' Viv said, staring at Ruddy.

He shrugged. 'You know the score. The fewer people who share information the safer it stays.'

Viv's mum stood up. 'Come on, Vivian, I'd like to get home. I've got a bridge four tonight that I don't want to miss.'

Viv raised her eyebrows, She had no idea her mum played bridge. 'When did that start?'

'Oh, my first week in the Pound.' She shot Viv a knowing look.

Viv, slightly rattled to hear her mum calling it that, smiled and went to open the door.

Mac got there ahead of her. 'Nice work, Mrs Fraser.'

'Oh Marcus, you can call me Trude.'

He said, 'I wouldn't dream of it, ma'am.'

As they passed through reception on the way back to the car, the doctor was hovering. She stepped forward and handed Viv a card. 'If you need anything.'

Viv took it instinctively and glanced at what was written on it – very little other than a name and a mobile number.

She tucked it into her jacket. 'Thanks, but hopefully she'll be fine now.'

Viv caught Mac and her mum smiling at each other.

'Something funny?'

Neither answered.

As they exited onto the lane at the back of Northumberland Street, Viv wondered at nosey neighbours who might question the goings in and out of this innocuous garage door. If she lived with a view of it she'd definitely have investigated it. She drove her mum back to her flat where Mand and James were waiting. Still no emotional reunion.

Viv said, 'I'll leave you to settle in, get a cup of tea with Mand.'

Her mum said, 'Come by tomorrow when James is at soft-play.'

Mand said, 'Ten 'til eleven-thirty.'

'Fine. See you then.'

As she and Mac walked toward the Rav he said, 'Are you guys for real? If my mum had been through such an ordeal we'd be all over her . . .'

'Aye, you hot blooded Italians cannae keep it to yersels.' She tapped his arm. 'Different strokes for different folks.'

'But you must feel like hugging her, surely?'

'It's not our way. However much one of us feels like it, it's not encouraged.'

He blew out a long breath. 'My God, in our family we almost kill each other with physical contact.'

'Can't be good for you.' She laughed. 'For your information, I did want to hug her, but she wouldn't have it. What was it you said about "old school"?' She glanced over at him in the passenger seat. 'Back to Doune?'

He said, 'Why not? Might as well get this thing wrapped up.'

'You know what I've learned from this?'

'No, tell me.'

'That I've got two mums; one who used to tell me that if I didn't pull my socks up I'd never play for Scotland, and the other who calls me Vivian in public and wouldn't let me touch her with a barge pole unless she was drowning. We are talking weird.'

'I never knew you played for Scotland.'

'I didn't. I literally wouldn't pull my socks up to full length or wear elastics to keep them in place, so I was dropped from the team. A sorry tale, but by that time I had other things on my mind.'

'Like what? What could be more important than playing for your country?'

She grinned at him. 'Oh God, use your imagination, I was eighteen.'

'How odd that I had no idea about any of that.'

'Look, if I know so little about my own mum, why should you know stuff about my teen years. You were with the big boys strutting your stuff.'

He snorted, 'You're confusing me with someone else. I'm a Marconi remember. Didn't make it into any of the strutting clubs. Longstone was such a divisive place.'

'Places can't be divisive, only people do that. Who kept you out? Anyone in particular?'

'Ironically, the Kellys. Nothing like a convert to light the evangelical torch. Mrs Kelly joined the Wee Frees. All things Catholic became the devil for her and boy did she massage that hatred into the boys.'

'Wow, I didn't know any of that was going on. So you see how much we don't know about each other, or those we thought we knew?'

'What d'you think she'll tell you tomorrow?'

'Who knows, but whatever it is will be a sanitised version of the truth. Pinch of salt and all that.' She shook her head. 'Did these last few days actually happen? Or did I dream it?'

He rubbed her arm. 'Oh, it was for real all right, you've even got the bruises to prove it.'

She sighed, 'What a marathon.'

'Imagine what life would have been like if you'd known what she was.'

'We probably wouldn't have believed it anyway. We'd have still told people she was a secretary. Come to think of it I don't think I ever told anyone that anyway. No one asked, not that I remember. Not convinced that my memory is up to much. I mean if I don't . . . if she had a broken rib how come we didn't know about that?'

'Might have been before you were born. She did have a life before you and Mand.'

She snorted, 'Yeah, we were late to her party . . . Just not getting my head round it. Maybe tomorrow will make a difference . . . but I doubt it. By the way did you ever get your own back on the Kellys?'

He laughed. 'Not me, but my sisters. They were, still are, supreme at humiliation. I'd never have dared do what they did.'

'Don't stop there, tell me.'

He shook his head. 'It's a punishable offence now.'

'Aw, please tell me.'

'No way. They're my team. A man never lets his team down.'

'I thought I was on your team.'

'You are, but a different one. Team Marconi . . .'

The nostalgia in his voice was comforting. Everyone needed people who would watch their back no matter what. Mac was probably as solid in himself as he was because of his family. She felt a stab of envy. She'd always thought of herself as having a good family, a good childhood, but maybe it had just been good enough. She needn't complain. So many people had a lot more to grumble about than not getting hugs.

Chapter Seventeen

Eventually back at the West Bow Viv had crawled into bed hoping that sleep would come. What she couldn't get her head around most was that her mum had, until the last week, behaved as if she was on a downhill trajectory; as if she was becoming a doddery old woman. Had that been an act or had that been Viv's interpretation of her life? They didn't see each other very often and when they did it was more often than not fractious. Maybe it was like that because Viv had made assumptions that riled her mum, or because they were too alike. No way. What about all those movies that she stared at? John Wayne for God's sake, who watched his films? She lay in bed and stared as the glow of car headlights scanned her walls. Her dad had watched any kind of action movie, so her mum probably watched them out of nostalgia, a way of staying connected to him. She punched her pillow into shape and tucked the duvet round her feet. Why were relationships more complicated than they looked, especially family ones? She'd made reasonable assumptions about her mum based on her behaviour. It had been a long time since they'd gone anywhere together. They didn't go out for lunch or on day trips. Mand was always doing stuff with her, even more since James came along. It was as if when she went to live in the Pound she'd given up. And why had she moved there anyway? Had she felt unsafe where she'd been? If so why? Was it to do with the work she'd been doing? The more Viv thought about all this the more distant her mum seemed. What had it cost her to have a double, perhaps triple life? She mused on her own situation. Having Sal, someone who worked in the same line of work, in her life eased the complication of having to hide what she was doing, although there were still some things they wouldn't talk to each other about. Had her mum and dad lived like that? Wow! The world was topsy-turvy. How could her family story have been so off the mark? The answer was of course because that was how her parents had wanted it. Normal, they wanted their kids to have as normal a life as possible, and the only way to do that was to build and maintain a narrative of ordinariness.

Wednesday

When sleep came it was fitful. She rose early and went out for a run. It was good to get out before she had to dodge the school kids on the streets. The Meadows had a few joggers and since the sun was making an effort to come through there were many 'good mornings' as they passed on their laps. She was a clockwise woman but there were those who were more comfortable with the opposite. Even in the most basic things folk were different. She smiled and increased her pace; it was okay to be different. How dull was sameness? Maybe she didn't need to know about her mum. Maybe it was best for her to go to her grave with those stories. After all they were her memories to keep.

When she arrived at the Pound Mand's car was already parked at the back door, so she pulled in behind it. Her mum answered the buzzer and the door clicked open. The warden was chatting to another resident and glanced at Viv, almost smiling before she realised who it was. Viv nodded and took the stairs. Her mum's door was ajar.

'Tea?' her mum said.

She'd have preferred coffee but said, 'Great.'

Mand shot her a look that she couldn't work out. Then she shrugged and Viv got the I've-no-idea-what's-going-on-here message.

Their mum brought a tray through with mugs, a pot of tea and a plate of plain digestives. 'Right, I suppose you want me to tell you all about my life in the service? Well, that's not going to happen. But what I will tell you is that during my time,' she poured out the tea and handed them each a mug, 'I had to look after an agent from another service. She for some reason left me a legacy in her will.'

Viv snorted. 'A bit of a . . .'

Her mum shot her a look. 'Do you want my story or not?'

Viv nodded and her mum continued, 'She left a large sum of money and a letter of wishes. In that letter she said that in the event of my death before the estate was wound up, the money was to go to the community. By this I assumed she meant the community that surrounded the camp that she was held in . . . where we were based. Locals were kind. They brought prisoners gifts of food, books, hand-knitted socks. So that's what I did. I created a trust for the community. They know best what they need. I had no idea she had sons. Otherwise . . .' she stared out of the window. 'Actually since she didn't change her will in their favour I'm guessing she had reason not to. So perhaps I'd have done exactly the same thing. And given Kristian and Kurt's recent behaviour she probably did have good reason. As for the other stuff for the service, I signed . . .'

Viv interrupted her, 'The Official Secrets Act.'

Her mum nodded. 'Exactly. And until I die it stays in here.' She tapped her temple. 'Disappointing for you two. I mean getting a little information is so tantalising, but you didn't get it from me and nor will you.'

Mand passed Viv the plate of digestives but she said, 'No thanks. I'll get something on my way home.'

Her mum said, 'Ever the independent.'

Viv grunted, 'Well, that's rich coming from you.'

Her mum stood at the window, straight-backed, almost elegant, or was it dignified? The way that she perceived her mum had changed, it had had to. The person she'd encountered in the last while bore no relation to the film-watching couch potato that she'd thought her mum had become.

She smiled at Mand. 'What do you think, sis?'

Mand sat with her mug in hand and was about to dip a digestive into it before stopping and laying it back on the plate, 'Well I'm sorry we're not getting to hear about your exploits, mum. I mean you are our mum.'

'And that's how I'd like it to stay. I don't need to be made into a superhero, because I'm not. I've always been your mum, the same mum whose home baking wasn't up to scratch for the school fair, but who won the egg and spoon race every year.' She sipped her tea, a smile creeping at the edges of her lips.

Viv had forgotten about school sports days, but now remembered that the other mums had talked about trying to beat her. They never had. How selective memories were. If she were to go through the family photograph albums now, knowing what little she did, she'd probably notice different things. She'd hatch a plan with Mand so that they could do it together. This episode was like finding out she'd had a long-lost brother or sister, a *Sliding Doors* moment, which left too many what ifs.

She laid her hands on her thighs and pushed herself up. 'If we're not getting the lowdown I've got things to do. How about you, Mand?' She glanced at her sister and saw her in a different light as well.

Mand raised her mug. 'I'll finish up here, but we'll speak later.'

Viv walked to her mum's side and felt her tense. She rubbed her upper arm. 'You've always been our superhero, Official Secrets Act or not.'

Her mum sighed, 'I wish your dad was here to see how grown up you both are.'

Viv turned and glanced at Mand who was wiping her cheek. 'Right I'll be off then.' She patted Mand's shoulder on the way to the door, but didn't look back.

She sprinted from the Grassmarket to the flat and took the stair two at a time. Her laptop was asleep but only took seconds to come to life. Her inbox pinged with message after message from Sal, as if they'd been in a holding cell for days. Good news, Sal was dying to hear her voice. She could do better than a phone call, so she Googled flights to New York. Sure enough, new direct flights to New York were available from Edinburgh. She might as well do it sooner rather than later. She clicked on the 'Buy Now' icon.

Viv grinned as she opened the fridge door. Not much of a selection but no point in stocking up now that she was going away. She threw open the sitting-room window and gazed at the hills in the distance. Time to find out what Sal was really up to.

THE END

Visit the links below for other books in the series.

For UK purchases go to - https://amzn.to/2thMEnb
For USA purchases go to - https://amzn.to/2THjudT

Be the first to know when V. Clifford's next book is available!
Follow her at
http://bookbub.com/authors/vclifford
to get an alert whenever she has a new release, preorder, or discount!

For further information or to sign up for news go to www.vclifford.com

Printed in Great Britain
by Amazon

44137658R00111